PRAISE FOR
Metropolitan Stories

"Every painting, every tapestry, every fragile, gilded chair in the Met not only has a story, but gets to tell it, in Christine Coulson's magical book. The history, humor, wonder, and—perhaps above all—beauty that Coulson absorbed in her twenty-five years at the museum burst forth from these pages."

——Ariel Levy, *The New Yorker* staff writer and *New York Times* bestselling author of *The Rules Do Not Apply*

"Written with elegance, wit, and a flair for comic genius, *Metropolitan Stories* describes the museum world as it is and as it strives to be. Coulson is a brilliant narrator of the fantastical. Her passion for art and her deep sense of human character make this not only a delightful book, but also a deeply rewarding one. It marks the emergence of a major new talent."

——Andrew Solomon, *New York Times* bestselling author of *The Noonday Demon* and *Far from the Tree*

"A truly magical book…This feels like a cross between *From the Mixed-Up Files of Mrs. Basil E. Frankweiler* and *Night at the Museum*."

——*Boston Magazine*

"[A] sly, whimsical debut…Those who think they know [the Met] will be beguiled by the look behind the scenes; those unfamiliar with it will be prompted to make its acquaintance."

——*Publishers Weekly*

METROPOLITAN STORIES

A Novel

Christine Coulson

Other Press / New York

First softcover edition 2021
ISBN 978-1-63542-093-7

Copyright © Christine Coulson 2019

Production editor: Yvonne E. Cárdenas
Text designer: Jennifer Daddio
This book was set in Centaur by
Alpha Design & Composition of Pittsfield, NH.

1 3 5 7 9 10 8 6 4 2

Library of Congress Cataloging-in-Publication Data

Names: Coulson, Christine, author.
Title: Metropolitan stories / Christine Coulson.
Description: New York : Other Press, 2019.
Identifiers: LCCN 2019007798 (print) | LCCN 2019000107 (ebook) |
ISBN 9781590510582 (hardcover) | ISBN 9781590510636 (ebook)
Subjects: LCSH: Metropolitan Museum of Art (New York, N.Y.)—Fiction.
Classification: LCC PS3603.O885 M48 2019 (ebook) | LCC PS3603.O885 (print) |
DDC 813/.6—dc23
LC record available at https://lccn.loc.gov/2019007798

Publisher's Note: This is a work of fiction. Names, characters, places,
and incidents either are the product of the author's imagination
or are used fictitiously.

WE

We protect them and save them and study them. After a time, we realize—some of us slower than others—that they are protecting us, saving us, studying us.

"We" are generations of golden children, thousands of staff members, raised by the Metropolitan Museum, put in its ward and shaped and stretched until our eyes can spot beauty like we're catching a ball, quick and needy, clutching it to our chests so it is ours, all ours.

Our knees buckle as we learn every one of the museum's tangled paths—every gallery, every limestone hall, every catwalk and shortcut, every stairway up and down and across and over—until our muscles, tutored and trained, always bend us in the right direction.

We dream of chalices and Rothkos, African masks and twisting Berninis unfolding in our minds like so many fluttering pages. Our hearts stutter with their stories, so many stories that words won't do. We need to show you what we see, what we have woken up, right here, right now, in this shiny box.

"They" are the objects, the art, the very stuff of the place. The things the public comes to see and longs for us to sing about, loudly and clearly and with every breath, until the visitors are too inspired, too tired, to see another bronze, another altarpiece, another sword or portrait or vase. After buying a bag of proof in the shop—a sack that says the museum has been done, with Van Gogh napkins to prove it—the visitors leave.

We and the objects stay. We have our evenings to cling together and our mornings to reunite. We connect like neighbors across a fence, one side always knowing more; we like to think it's us, but it's them. Our hungry scholarship scratches for what they've already lived. Those objects were there, saw the whole thing, right in front of them. Watched the tomb door close, pinching the sunlight until it narrowed to one last blinding stripe, then *thrrump!* Gone.

We depend upon their magic, know it like a quiet superstition. The objects glide into our world—once fixed, now moving—each time showing up somewhere we did not expect. Because we did not realize that we needed to be rescued by marble and silk, or canvas and oil paint, or charcoal upon a page, pushing beyond gilded frames and glass cases to reach out and do with us what they will, always for good. Never against us. Those works of art *work*—to make the right things happen and sweep the wrong things down the steps of the museum in heavy drips that collect and wash away. And we are breathless and relieved to have the art on our side. It is why we never leave.

CHAIR AS HERO

Sometimes I wish we had a support group. We would start by introducing ourselves.

"Hi, I'm a fauteuil à la reine made for Louise-Élisabeth, Duchess of Parma."

The other chairs would immediately think I'm an asshole, particularly the older Windsor chairs.

Everyone would know that I still have my original upholstery and that I've made cameo appearances in a few minor paintings. There's some cred in that, but also a lot of resentment.

I remember back in Paris when a master carver sculpted me into coils and tendrils, decoration so florid that even my smoothest surface arched into acrobatic movement: swinging, reaching, bounding, wrapping with wisteria determination.

Gold leaf coated each of these spiraling forms. The sheets of the precious metal, impossibly thin, floated onto my exposed wood like a soft rain, cool and tender. Silk velvet was then stretched across my curves, a fine, bespoke suit, taut and precise, with glistening ornament along its edges.

I can picture Louise-Élisabeth's daughter, Isabella, age eight, on the day I arrived from France at the Ducal Palace of Colorno in Parma. It was 1749, and she stroked my crimson velvet with such care, trying to appear grown up and sophisticated.

But I also remember when she curled herself within my arms and cried fat, messy tears, her knees tucked tightly beneath the panniers of her gown with its flowers and ribbons. I can still feel the heaving of her chest against my back as she shivered gently to the rhythm of her sobs. How I wish I could have swayed along with that pulsing sorrow to comfort her.

Only five years later, Isabella's siblings, Ferdinand and Maria Luisa, would topple into me during audiences with their parents and pull at my gold trimmings, as clumsy and silly as any children, despite their finery.

One time at the Met, a small boy—not more than three years old—wandered past the barriers in the Wrightsman Galleries and headed straight for me. Almost two hundred and twenty-five years had passed, but he reminded me so much of those toddlers back in Parma.

Come on little guy! I thought from behind the gallery ropes. *You can make it!*

The boy's plump hands extended forward, propelled by his thick, tumbling waddle, his shoes clomping on the gallery floor. I felt like I was hanging from a cliff waiting for him to grip my arm and save me. Then a breeze of moist heat floated past as his mother grabbed him at the very last second—just before he reached me.

That was 1978. I still dream about it. I imagine the boy climbing up onto my seat. His pleasant folds and warm, springy pudge nestled between my arms. A small puddle of drool soaking into my velvet, the life of it racing through to my frame.

I would share those dreams in the meetings.

Of course, I remember the lonely attics and warehouses, too. Rooms of swollen heat and shrinking cold. Dark, hollow, airless. A desolate purgatory, despite the stacked and crowded landscape, a bulging mountain range of the stored and forgotten.

In the brittle stillness, dust showered down upon me with a fragile constancy, like some gray and final mist, ashen drifts accumulating on my every surface. For decades, I ached for the feel of footsteps rattling through the floorboards, quivering up my legs, delivering some—any—faint agitation of life. And oh, to be the chosen one when that door finally swung open, the chooser blackened against the blaze of ripe and glorious light!

Storage would definitely come up in the meetings, too.

Eventually I landed back in Paris at Maison Leys, the city's foremost interior decorating firm at the turn of the century. There, in 1906, the legendary connoisseur Georges Hoentschel sold me to the American giant J.P. Morgan, along with two thousand other pieces of furniture. Morgan gave the whole lot of us to the Met, where I will always live in great splendor.

But Parma was my home. I will never forget the light and shadow of those glorious rooms of my youth. Some days I trace every detail in my mind, the way prisoners do to survive captivity. I feel Louise-Élisabeth's body collapsing onto me, tired and alone: the fearless daughter of a king, frustrated by her timid spouse and hindering lack of beauty. I can still smell the sour odor of her flaccid husband as he picked at my gilding.

Little Maria Luisa eventually became Queen of Spain after she was engaged to her cousin Charles at age eleven. Short and not as pretty as her older sister, her feet swung lazily from my edge as she listened to her mother explain the arrangements of the loveless marriage. As rebellion or consolation, a parade of lovers would later sink into my velvet during Maria Luisa's reign.

Maria Luisa kept me with her until she died in Rome in 1819. I held her through the fear and tragedy of twenty-four pregnancies over twenty-eight years. Only six babies survived.

I wouldn't talk about those memories in the meetings.

MUSING

The briefing memo was clear: "Mr. Lager-feld will bring his Muse. The Muse will not speak. Do *not* address the Muse."

Michel read the sentences twice. He did not relish the idea of meeting with a fashion de-signer, but found himself curiously admiring this par-ticular detail. It had been a long time since anyone had truly surprised him. He wondered why he himself had never thought of such an accessory.

Michel's twenty-eight-year career had been marked by the acquisition of every stylish trapping: a baroque desk, volumes of art books, handmade suits each punctuated by his small, red Chevalier lapel marker. But a Muse. Ah, the cleverness of bringing a Muse to a meeting. Michel took the eccentric gesture as both an invitation and a challenge. As the Director of the greatest museum in the world, he could surely scare up a Muse by tomorrow.

Maybe an attractive curator, he thought to himself, his mind racing through the staff to inventory the possibilities. Rather paltry, he smirked. Didn't it use to be different? He remembered a time when the Met seemed to be riddled with alluring women targeting his handsome affection. Had the gay men taken over? Or did he just not notice as much anymore?

The Drawings Department had an intriguing brunette researcher, and that Italian decorative arts curator always made him think of eighteenth-century French novellas about sex and exquisite furniture.

That startlingly good-looking woman in Finance would do. He always felt a minor frisson when she rode the elevator with him. Astonishing legs, even in flat shoes—which he never liked. He had been known to summon her for a spurious budget question on a slow afternoon. But even he would be hard-pressed to justify her attendance at a meeting with a fashion designer.

Lily Martin would be there, but the Museum's President, while striking, functioned more like a sister than a Muse. She didn't have the right *éclat*—and there was certainly no telling *her* not to speak.

Eleanor would figure it out.

"Elllleanooor!" he bellowed in his signature baritone, "I will need a Muse for my meeting with Karl Lagerfeld tomorrow."

"Of course," Eleanor replied without enthusiasm. She occupied a gray cubicle outside Michel's office and, after twenty-four years as his assistant, very little could get her out of her seat, least of all his demand for a Muse.

"We'll need someone raaaavishing." Michel continued, still shouting from inside his office. He prolonged the pronunciation of the last word with particular thrust.

Again, Eleanor was unfazed. Unlike Michel, she skipped any consideration of the staff and went right to the art. Plenty of Muses there. Surely they could ask a Muse from the collection to attend an hour-long meeting.

She remembered when the figures from Rembrandt's self-portraits abandoned their paintings and came over to the office to hold Michel's hand through his sixty-fifth birthday. *That* was a long day. Eleanor never told anyone about the sobbing she heard behind Michel's door as he confronted that milestone. You wouldn't expect Rembrandt's old boys to be so empathetic, but they sat with him for hours. They understood Michel's vulnerability—had felt it all before themselves—and misery does love a little camaraderie.

Eleanor wouldn't mention that, historically speaking, a Muse does the picking, not the other way around. This detail need not apply to Michel Larousse, who tended to be self-inspired. She understood him well enough to see that this project was an amusement, a mildly competitive way of making a fashion designer look foolish by participating in his charade.

She also knew that Michel was getting tired in a more fundamental way, and that these spasms of some central, fading self were a way of holding on. She looked down and slowly shook her head, thinking of a former curator's description of Michel many years ago: "He just loves to be that *special* boy."

The scramble began. There were things that Michel did not care about (the public, unattractive people, American art, the Education Department) and those that were critical (European paintings, beautiful women, the rich, the absence of oregano in any meal). A showdown of Muses would fall definitively into the latter category and would be subject to a connoisseur's rigor.

An unspoken requirement was that the Muse not outshine her inspiree. Certainly, great beauty was required, but there were limits. The selected Muse would be strumming her lyre for a man with a special spotlight in his office that subtly illuminated him in his chair. She should be an exceptional ornament, but could not divert attention from the Director himself. It was a delicate balance.

Eleanor started by calling the Greek and Roman Department to see if this task could be dispensed with quickly. They immediately sent up *The Three Graces*. But the Graces were naked, headless, and inextricably linked together, so she sent them back. They shuffled out clumsily, the stuttering steps of the conjoined, silent in their headless disappointment.

Eleanor knew the collection held plenty of Muses—a popular subject throughout art history—so she flexed the power of the Director's Office and had a junior assistant hand-deliver an urgent memo to the heads of all seventeen curatorial departments:

THE METROPOLITAN MUSEUM OF ART
INTERDEPARTMENTAL MEMORANDUM

TO: Curatorial Department Heads
FROM: Eleanor Rock, Director's Office
RE: Urgent Request

January 26, 1998

It has come to our attention that the Director will need a Muse for a meeting tomorrow. Please send all applicable candidates to the Director's Office by 10:30 AM today. Beauty and condition should be strong considerations in your selection. Thank you.

Eleanor was fully aware of the chaos she was igniting. Before long, the Director's Office looked like a production of *A Chorus Line*. Muses of every stripe, stroke, and stipple crowded the waiting area and spilled out into the hallway, gathering in confused clumps, many creakingly stiff, frozen in their original poses. It had been a long time since they'd moved.

Some departments stretched the definition of Muse quite radically, but many of the collection's Muses could be traced back to the original myth of Zeus's nine daughters, each inspiring within a particular discipline: Calliope (epic poetry), Clio (history), Erato (love poetry), Euterpe (lyric poetry), Melpomene (tragedy), Polyhymnia (sacred poetry), Terpsichore (dance), Thalia (comedy), and Urania (astronomy).

"I hear this guy's a real creep," one Melpomene sputtered.

"Really?" an Erato responded, tuning her lyre. "I heard he's hot."

"A total god," chimed in a Polyhymnia.

"Apparently, he's seduced every good-looking woman in the building," a Clio added.

"Well, *she* must have enjoyed that," a Thalia snorted sarcastically.

And so the nervous chatter went, not just between these Muses but among their many sisters—there were thirteen Calliopes and another fifteen Clios and nearly twenty Thalias, and it went on with more and more joining by the minute. Because there had never been such a need—an open call for help from the collection—there was no sense of the protocol.

One nineteenth-century porcelain Thalia felt unaccountably nervous in the face of this undefined process. She remembered being scrutinized in 1982 by the museum's Acquisitions Committee, who would decide whether or not she should be purchased for the collection. Many a gloved hand inspected her before a valiant Met curator championed her cause, citing her as a "magical display of hard-paste porcelain frivolity." She wasn't that expensive, so most of the Trustees were willing to acquiesce, but one held firm. The formidable board member, Cordelia Wilmington, passed a note to the Committee Chairman that simply read: "Dog." It was only later revealed that Mrs. Wilmington's father had run off with a woman who looked strikingly similar to the figurine.

Most of the Muses had entered the collection in the early days of the Met, when Muses were fashionable and the museum would take any art it was offered. The American Wing's Miss Morse, a.k.a. *The Muse* (oil on canvas by Samuel F. B. Morse, ca. 1836–37), had been around since 1945. Now, sitting in the Director's Office, Miss Morse looked overdressed in her nineteenth-century taffeta gown, a stiff mustard-colored confection with a large belt and extravagant lace collar. Next to all the diaphanous fabric, she appeared to be shielding herself from something fierce and threatening.

"I'm not even sure why I'm here," Miss Morse observed aloud. "Is this some sort of exhibition in the making?" Her voice trilled the sound of an untroubled life, of a woman protected and consumed by the pursuits of her needlework and sketchbook.

"No, sweetie," chomped a showgirl version of Calliope from the European Paintings collection. As she spoke, she fluttered her eyelashes, which looked as though they might disconnect and flit away like dragonflies. "The museum's Director needs a Muse.

We're all here to help. It's a real honor, sweetie." The word "honor" was pronounced "on-nah," punctuated by more rhythmic flaps of her lashes.

"What if one does not care to participate?" inquired Miss Morse. "I do not work."

"Eh, Muse's dilemma, right? Always on call." Calliope shrugged her shoulders in a modern gesture of "get over it" that Miss Morse did not understand.

"Quite," she replied, merely to end the exchange.

In response to the chaos of this new sorority, Eleanor recruited help from the Development Office, where one could always find clipboard-clutching young women trained to assemble and organize.

They began by dividing the Muses into groups by their names, but then, remembering who would ultimately be receiving them, thought better of it. This would be a largely superficial endeavor. And so, for efficiency, the Muses were arranged first by curatorial department (the Director had his favorites) and then by hair color (the Director had his favorites).

Other elements came into play. For example, Muses who could only lean left or right, having been positioned that way for centuries. The left-leaners sloped against the far wall while the right-leaners formed a line along the bookcase. They might have been weeded out from the start, but the leaners were some of the most beautiful and thinly dressed. Michel would want to see them.

Some of the Muses seemed to have their own wind source that sent their gowns swirling and left their hair artfully tousled. Others were almost bone-less in their need for languor, draped limply across office furniture as if they were somehow melting. A few love-poem girls had Cupid in tow and played their lyres endlessly, making the office feel like a lin-gerie department before Valentine's Day. The trag-edy bunch was solemn and defeated, clutching their frown-faced masks with deflated resignation. No one could really tell the epic poets from the sacred poets, but the lyric poets could be found rhyming like dainty rappers. The dancers stretched. The as-tronomy ladies played constellation games, while the comedians just annoyed everyone by barking jokes among themselves.

"Hey Eleanor, what do you call a Muse who can't stand up straight?"

"Eileen," Eleanor answered back flatly, unamused. She'd heard them all.

Most of the Development staff rolled their eyes at this entire endeavor, despite the priority always placed on the Director's needs.

Daphne, a Development veteran of fourteen years, may have been the sole person who enjoyed these assignments and their proximity to the great man. Michel intimidated and frightened her, but a surprising humanity would sometimes flash from behind his celebrated persona. He seemed to understand the fear he instilled in others and respected the courage it took for someone in Daphne's position to play along with him, especially at times like this. When he said thank you, it was never as small as *thanks*. It carried the weight of real gratitude, the heft of a withholding father at a moment of crackling sentiment.

Staring at the pile of women in the waiting room, Daphne remembered when, a decade earlier, a Jordanian sheik had brought all his wives along with him to deliver a stunning amount of cash in several briefcases. "They all just sat there in silence while we judged them, and they judged us," she recalled to her younger colleague Jamie.

"The Muses don't seem to judge," Jamie replied, watching the disorder worsen. "They're more pushy than judge-y. More demanding, like 'Get inspired. Now.'" Indeed, there was a kind of amateur urgency among the Muses, a frantic desire to get the job done that made their grace simultaneously buoyant and desperate.

Eleanor emerged from Michel's office. "He's ready," she said, without further explanation.

The inner sanctum of the Director's Office was a book-lined cave with surprisingly little art in residence. The overall impression was neither grand nor timid. Rather, it achieved that most elusive of design effects: the air of inevitability. Of course Michel was here doing this job in this office. One could not imagine the room any other way or with any other occupant.

A large Canaletto painting of eighteenth-century Venice hung over a tired velvet sofa meant for courtiers who did not belong at the expansive conference table. At the other end of the room was a grand desk, tucked within a bay of windows designed like the command station of a ship. A leather office chair rolled behind the desk, but no other chairs sat opposite.

The strategy was simple, and effective: Make them stand. Michel found that enforced standing made interactions brief and more focused. Allowing someone a chair hinted that he might be interested in their views on a variety of topics when, in fact, he usually just wanted them to leave.

Not so today. The auditioning of nearly one hundred Muses was a delightful distraction from the approving or disapproving of mediocre ideas that usually consumed his morning.

Daphne appeared in the doorway and outlined the system that they had developed in the waiting room: groupings according to curatorial department and hair color. She knew this would allow them to move quickly through Michel's least favorite department. "Shall we start alphabetically with the American Wing, sir?"

"If we must," he replied with a hint of sarcasm. He was aware of and appreciated the considerable efforts made to keep him happy. Over the past two and a half decades, the museum had grown around his interests and desires, conforming to them like a well-worn shoe, creased and cleft by the repetition of his opinions, so often delivered in the same direction. Like aged leather, thickened by its wear, the result was a stronger museum. He and it, man and institution, had fused into a single entity.

A major crease in the shoe was Michel's long-held disinterest in American art, reaffirmed when Miss Morse entered the room.

"Good morning Mr. Larousse. I believe there has been some mistake," she began.

"Who are *you*?" Michel was startled by the sight of a prim nineteenth-century woman holding a sketchbook and wearing an enormous yellow dress.

"Susan Walker Morse," she replied in a diminutive voice. "I'm titled *The Muse*, so I suspect that is why I have been brought forward in this way, but I think you will agree that a return to the galleries would not only be appropriate, but a suitable response to my misdirected invitation? I do not think I can be helpful to you at this time."

"Indeed," Michel agreed, already looking over her shoulder as he thought to himself, *this is not* at all *what I had in mind.*

The next American muse turned out to be quite sizable, a hulking Statue of Liberty hung with drapery as thick as the drop cloths they used to protect the floors when the galleries were painted. She held a paintbrush and slumped herself down heavily on top of the conference table; now seated, the outlines of the dense fabric revealed knees the size of soccer balls. Again, this was not what Michel had envisioned.

"Elllleanooor!"

No instructions were needed. Despite the efficiency of the Development Office, they were unaccustomed to the more delicate needs of the Director. A large, brooding woman from the American Wing would require instant removal. Eleanor guided the giant, stiffly draped Muse from the room like a nurse tending to an aged patient.

Michel raised an eyebrow at this unwelcome display; an American Muse was an oxymoron to him anyway. "Perhaps we should move on to the next department..." he said to Eleanor as she was leaving.

Daphne returned to announce that the Drawings and Prints Department would be next. "They are all grisaille, sir, so hair color didn't much come into play."

Michel recognized the earnest delivery of this information, but also enjoyed the ridiculousness of it. "Perhaps we can see the gray ladies as a group, then."

As requested, thirty-eight women in various states of completion entered the room. Many were leaners, eager to find some architectural feature with which they could support themselves. Others were nearly naked, only a few lines here and there representing their drapery. The engravings were particularly graphic with their bold cross-hatching and piercing linearity. What united them was their exposure: each had something fleshy revealed—a breast, a shoulder, a bare leg, an uncovered back—while some piece of fabric tumbled off their body. It should have had the air of a goddess convention, but instead it was like an old black-and-white photo of a lewd debutante ball, with some sections wildly out-of-focus.

"No," Michel said with the frustrated disappointment of a boy who was expecting a pony for his birthday and got socks instead. The thirty-eight women would quietly return to their acid-free boxes, sealed from the light and air and bugs that continually threatened their survival. They would not remember their audience fondly.

European Paintings followed, first with a sullen Corot in a long, burlap vest and plain skirt; she could only look down and to the side, as if she were cheating on a math test. But she was French and from a favored department, so despite these limitations she had her (very brief) viewing. The Calliope with the extravagant eyelashes then entered with swinging hips, only to be met with the arched brows and dipping chin of Michel's wide-eyed disapproval.

"The big guy's gotta take me as I am, hun," she shrugged toward Eleanor as she left.

The nervous porcelain Thalia came in next. Michel smiled to himself remembering the "Dog" note from Mrs. Wilmington and the scandalous story behind it. The comedy Muse had luster, but was too foolish for his needs, and Michel was wise enough to know that his Trustees' desires far outweighed his own.

He dismissed the small pale woman, who was followed by a ceramic group of all nine muses in matching blue and orange costumes. They were sixteenth-century Italian, jolly and good-humored, a colorful squad of cheerleaders before a big game. Un-prompted, they sat around the conference table as if they had borrowed the room for a meeting. Michel sensed that he should join them, just to be polite, when Apollo entered. His manner was part manager, part pimp as he cast blinding sunlight across the room. The Muses seemed relieved that he had joined them.

Daphne approached Michel and spoke softly to give him some background. "There is some concern among the group that they *not* be separated. They are part of an inkstand that was broken up long ago and repaired. They fear they will be divided again. Apollo seems to be in charge."

Michel nearly slammed his head on the desk, but took a deep breath instead, before summoning his deepest voice, "*in aeternum unitum.*" Daphne did not speak Latin, but grasped enough to usher the group out like they had finished visiting the Oval Office for a photo-op with the President.

"Daphne, is that all from ESDA?" Michel asked when she reached the door. The acronym for

European Sculpture and Decorative Arts was pronounced "ehz-dah."

"Yes," Daphne responded. "I took the liberty of rejecting the bronze astronomy muse for excessive drapery."

"Very well," Michel said. He enjoyed the fact that actions were always taken to satisfy his robust reputation, however apocryphal it was. This mythology about him took little effort to maintain and at times seemed to describe a completely separate being: a vain lion who reveled in both his own image and his unrivaled conquests as he diminished everyone around him. Some days he, too, felt as though he worked for Michel Larousse. Or that he needed to zip himself into a Michel Larousse Suit to play the character that everyone expected.

Daphne nervously looked down at her clipboard to refer to her notes without a real need to do so. "Greek and Roman is next. Naturally they are the biggest group. I've divided them into two sets: the broken ones and the ones from the Greek vases."

"Bring in the broken group. I imagine that will be brief."

Daphne left the office and Michel found himself slumped in his chair wondering how a day of certain delight had devolved into such tedium. An hour into this process and he had had no fun at all. Had this been a bad idea, crafting this…this pageant? Or had he wanted something more—not just a talisman of beauty, but a more potent refueling after twenty-eight years?

The broken horde arrived. Missing were mainly noses and arms with a couple of bad restorations reminding him of the questionable plastic surgery of some of his Trustees.

In the early days of the museum, curators and restorers were not shy about putting a new nose—or a random ancient nose—on a statue where one was missing. It never worked: The parts were fine individually, but the whole didn't make sense as a face. Michel thought that was how some of his Board members looked, with their pinched skin and restored features. It was as if they had gone into the museum's storeroom and picked out some fresh, often unsympathetic parts to retrieve an ill-advised and unavailable youth.

Like those Trustees, the broken Muses retained an aura of lost beauty, the veil of an exquisite past that hung on them despite their current condition. Michel rarely acknowledged his nostalgia for his own lost beauty, but it was there, and informed much of his behavior. Age had arrived like twilight, slowly and unnoticed. But he resisted its recognition. The Michel Larousse Suit was made in the image of the Young Michel, with his devastating movie-star looks and unshakable swagger. It was an easier fit, and more compelling.

He thought of Lucian Freud, that master of flesh who documented the ravages of aging so brutally. What Freud could do with him now, Michel wondered.

As his thoughts lingered, he realized that he had spent a fair amount of time staring at the broken women, who were starting to look uncomfortable.

"Told you he was weird," whispered one.

"Total creep," hissed another.

"Freak," mouthed a third.

Michel became aware of the awkwardness and responded with reflexive arrogance. At these moments, he never called upon the person directly involved in the situation, but instead returned to the security of Eleanor.

"Elllleanooor!" She appeared in the doorway, and the broken women turned to her with a look that said, "Get. Us. Out. Of. Here."

No words were needed as she resumed her role as nurse, escorting the collection of wounded creatures past both her desk and Daphne, and back into the hallway.

"There you go," Eleanor said curtly. It was her way of saying goodbye.

Daphne looked confused and concerned that she had made some fundamental error. Eleanor then turned to her and took control. "We'll skip the fifth-century Greeks. Too flat for his mood. Who's left?"

The Modern Department stepped far afield of tradition, offering Brancusi's sleeping Muse who was without a body, along with Picasso's portraits of his Muses, known as "the weeping women." Michel rejected them solely on Daphne's hesitant description. Like many men, Michel had been known to cave to a crying woman, but not on this project. Their wails and grievances about the great master would be merely tiresome, reminding him of the assistant they once had in the office who cried whenever her memos were edited.

Michel had certainly been present when more than one donor had broken into tears upon seeing their name on a gallery wall. Not out of pride, but because of the tombstone look of the thing. It was a common but unexpected response. He had learned long ago not to comfort the rich. They paid others for that. Even if the looming end to his own long reign made him feel a similar dread. He knew how many pages were left in his book as if the thing itself sat in his hands, waiting to be finished. So he read more slowly, almost sounding out the words to make the paragraphs last longer.

Only the Department of Photographs remained. There had been some crying in the creation of that department. Its chairman—a tiny, determined woman—battled with Michel like Muhammad Ali fought George Foreman: She took her punches early and often, hanging on until Michel was exhausted. It was no easy sell separating Photographs from the Prints Department, where they were all considered works on paper. But there she had stood, white-knuckled in the face of all arguments. He had always admired her re-solve, though he withheld that approbation.

Michel was about to yell for Eleanor when his of-fice door whipped open and banged against the wall. The silhouette of a tall, stark-naked woman appeared. There were no accessories for this candidate save the fur-lined high-heeled shoes she wore. A stunning clas-sical profile was framed by the short, slick waves of her hair.

"What department are *you* from?" Michel asked, eager to get this one started. She was the only Muse he had spoken to since Miss Morse.

"Photographs," she replied with a French accent he guessed was Swiss. "Meret Oppenheim. The so-called Muse to the Surrealists?" She uttered this last statement disparagingly, hinting at her resentment of the title and suggesting that perhaps Michel was too uninformed to know who she was.

Her skin was matte, a glowing white surface that you could almost crack and peel like a hard-boiled egg. She was not quite of this earth, but instead had a luminescence interrupted only by the tuft of dark hair between her legs.

Magnetic and bold, she sat on the conference table and used two chairs to support her feet, one for each shoe. Then she opened her knees and revealed herself to him, leaning forward in the pose of an athlete in the locker room at half-time.

"A Muse, huh?" she laughed lightly, implying that this was a child's game. Unlike others, she could distinguish between Michel and his constructed façade.

"The fur teacup," Michel said urgently, citing her most famous work of art, as if he were being quizzed. *"Le Déjeuner en fourrure."*

"Exactement." The object defined her. She had grown to loathe the iconic tea cup, the product of a whimsical café conversation with Picasso.

Michel enjoyed her power and its intimidation. How her bright moon eclipsed his sun. The sense that in her presence, it was *her* role to do the work, to be in charge, maybe even frighten him a little. He didn't need a Muse. He didn't need inspiration. He didn't need to toy with a fashion designer's farce. He needed her searing force to replace his slow, simmering fatigue. He needed the comfort of someone else's strength.

Finally, he thought, leaning back in his chair. "Ravishing," he sighed. "Ravishing."

Eleanor instinctively knew that the chore was complete and instructed Daphne to send any lingering Muses back to their various galleries and storerooms. She then picked up the phone to call Moody Russell, her favorite lamper. The bulb in Michel's special spotlight was beginning to flicker.

MEATS & CHEESES

Oh, hurrah! You've arrived." The bald man behind a wide desk held up his hands and clapped them once in satisfaction. The accent was patrician, but friendly. "You must be here for the meat."

"The what?" I asked. I looked back at the dark ramp I had just ascended from within the museum to the sun-drenched room where I now stood.

As my eyes adjusted to the brightness, I could see through the window behind the bald man. A colonnade led to an expanse of blistering desert, an infinite sweep of sand that burned its harsh radiance into my eyes.

"Right. Jolly-ho," the man continued, ignoring my question. "Shut the door behind you, dear," he said with a flick of his hand in the air. "Helen!" he yelled to the next room, "A girl's here for the meat!"

I closed the blue door as he fumbled with stacks of papers spread across the broad oak desktop. I noticed his high-waisted khaki trousers and pale bow tie, both smudged with dirt, rough but elegant.

Hats of all kinds hung from hooks along the white stucco wall: pith helmets, straw boaters, woven bonnets neatly wrapped with pale ribbons. All bore the tired cast of long wear and frequent use. A faded World War I campaign hat, broad-brimmed and pinched symmetrically at its four corners, was stenciled with the name WINLOCK.

"Oh, bubbly boo...it was *right here*. Hellll-en!!" the man yelled again.

From behind a curtained doorway emerged an old-fashioned looking woman in a loose dress, the white cotton marred with smudges similar to those on the man's pants. Her hair was pinned close to her head in neat waves. Sand crunched beneath her laced-up shoes as she walked.

"What is it, Hebe? Why are you making such a racket?" she said.

They both spoke with the clipped speed of another era.

"Oh, hullo," she said, looking at me, "You must be here for the meat. Lovely."

"Exactly," Hebe replied, still moving things from place to place. He swung his head back to me as he leaned over the table and gestured with his chin toward a wooden chair. "Have a seat, why don't you. This won't take but a minute. The meat is here somewhere. How you lose a four-thousand-year-old leg of lamb I'm not sure...we have it, we must...we do...well, somewhere."

"Hebe, wasn't it in an envelope in the library?" Helen asked.

"Was it?" he responded, still flipping through folders and books, the sound of the sand's grit scratching beneath his feet. "I thought I had it right here last week?"

The prospect of ancient meat held little allure, but these people and their flickering presence were riveting, like watching an old black-and-white film. I took a seat on the chair in the corner and listened to the trill of their banter, not sure what I had come upon. Just minutes before, I had been in the tunnels of the Met—the grim bowels below the basement where storage cages made with woven-metal fencing held retired art and cartons of old paperwork. A blue door had brought me to a room at the edge of the desert and to a time that was definitely *not* 1995.

I was an assistant in the Met's Development Office, which I both belonged to and observed, like a natural wonder staged for remote viewing. Within this fundraising habitat I ranked as the lowest species: a phone-answering, errand-running assistant. When not traversing the museum, I sat on a stool.

I had only worked at the Met for a year, but its strange cocktail of confident superiority and tolerated eccentricity had introduced me to a promised land. A position to deploy my quick, organized mind in the service of a place that left me both exhilarated and soothed.

I wore my grandmother's old suits, the skirts lopped off to make sense on my young frame, and bought one pair of good shoes that I only wore inside the museum.

From my stool, I watched, listened, and learned. Ideas were "run up the flagpole," letters signed with "kind regards," satisfied requests described as "deposits in the favor bank." The language and routines of the museum's staff fascinated me, and I collected their habits like so many butterflies.

These were my people, and I wanted in.

Our office had one telephone line connected to thirty-five phones, so when anyone called, it collectively rang at thirty-five desks. Everyone called: donors, curators, caterers, the White House. All day. My colleagues and I responded with unflappable spirit, taking diligent messages on small sheets of blue paper that documented each call, daily field notes on scribbled rectangles.

I escaped this clamoring switchboard when I was asked to deliver "cheeses," yellow envelopes with holes in them that were used for the Met's interoffice mail. I charged through the museum—quick and nimble, my arms and legs as skinny as bare branches—carrying the yellow envelopes to intimidating men and women, then waiting for their signature to mark their approval of the documents inside.

It was a typical Tuesday when I was asked to shepherd a cheese to the most daunting recipient of them all.

"Dick Trachner's Office," Susan answered the phone, with a level of cheer greatly at odds with the man she represented.

"Susan, it's Kate. I need to get Mr. Trachner's sign-off on the title-wall design for the China exhibition," I said, already anxious.

"Sure! Just cheese it to me," she squeaked.

"I'd better not. If I bring it over in a cheese, can you get him to sign it while I wait?"

"Of course! You can bring it to him yourself!"

Susan maintained a helpful stance, but I suspected that underneath all her sunshine lay a cruel streak, a woman who enjoyed watching young assistants interact with her boss's frightening intensity. A small group of outsized figures like Trachner ran the Metropolitan and intrigued us all. Each employed a seasoned gatekeeper who deftly maintained power with a persona that skewed both warm and ominous.

"Go on in!" Susan said when I arrived, barely containing her feline amusement.

"Right now?" I asked.

"Well, you said you needed it signed…," she purred.

"Right. OK."

I entered the legendary office where Dick Trachner sat—rigid, scrutinizing, impenetrable—as if he had been watching the door for my arrival all morning.

I had heard about the office: as spare as a monk's cell, but with a more sinister quality to it. No papers, no decorations. Instead, the Senior Vice President for Operations sat behind a large gray desk that supported only a phone and an enormous red ashtray.

"Hi," he said breathily, his teeth fully exposed as he clamped on the word. He spoke as if addressing a toddler.

"Good morning," I replied, pulling the design for the title wall from its cheese and pointing to where it needed to be signed.

Standing over him, I confronted the reality of his bald head, its polymer-like surface populated by baby-fine spikes of hair, enduring weeds in an otherwise barren field. I squinted in revulsion at his scalp's pockmarks and flaking skin.

"Well, all-righty then...," he said. He looked at the design as he tortured me with the leisurely uncapping of his pen. "There you go. Signed, sealed, and delivered."

"Thank you, Mr. Trachner," I replied while stepping out of the room.

"Kate," he said in a low voice he knew I would still hear.

I shuddered at the fact that Dick Trachner knew my name and re-entered his office as if I were checking on a basement noise in a horror film.

"I need you to do me a favor. After you drop off those designs, tell Libby that you have to pick something up in the tunnels. Susan will tell you where it is."

"Tell Libby" seemed like an ambitious directive. Libby was my boss, and I had never seen anyone of my rank "tell Libby" anything. Libby told *you* what to do and when to do it—period. As for the tunnels, I knew they existed, but had never been in them.

Trachner's instructions hung in the air, spare and intentionally vague, waiting for my response. The request would annoy Libby, but I was pretty sure that no one said no to Dick Trachner. Staff-Cafeteria lore claimed him as both CIA *and* FBI.

Smoke curled around his head as he waited for my response.

"Will do, Mr. Trachner," I answered with a strange gesture that came close to a thumbs-up. I embarrassingly realized the position of my hand, and slowly deflated the thumb.

"Thank you," he said with false sincerity, enjoying my lack of knowledge and obvious discomfort.

In my snappy suits and high heels, Trachner understood that I was dressed for a part that I didn't play. A straight-A nerd with style and speed, I had something to prove, but didn't know what it was. He could smell my overeagerness and would enjoy testing it.

And I was delighted to be in the game.

Susan drew the directions on a notepad with a Sharpie and handed the map to me with a knowing smile. "Look for the blue door," she said, purring again. "Good luck."

I returned the signed title-wall design to the Development Office and was relieved to see Libby's door closed for a meeting. I left quickly and took the Wing K elevators down past the ground floor.

Unlike the hive of the museum's basement, the tunnels are lifeless. They stretch and curl in unpredictable patterns under arched brick ceilings that run the length of the museum, lined with pipes and electrical wiring. I didn't see another soul when I was down there. I only heard the buzzing of the fluorescent lights above me. An occasional fan whirred with a dull drone.

I crawled along the path outlined on Susan's paper map, passing demoted statuary lurking below the angled ducts and curving architecture. Other statues looked upward as if longing to return to the galleries, light raking across their faces to emphasize their yearning. In the swelling gray gloom, I shared their desire as I sank deeper into the cluttered passageways—at once constricting and vast.

I passed a marble sculpture of a woman, buoyant as an apparition, striding toward the tunnel wall in flowing robes. I half expected her to travel through the brick. Beyond her, a group of tall medieval figures shrouded in thick plastic glinted abstract shapes out of the shadows. More ghosts.

In the cage for the Greek and Roman Department, I saw shelves of retired pieces of antique sculpture— noses, feet, hands—bits once used a century ago to replace a statue's missing parts. The tunnels' dusty quiet settled around me, and I thought about the Met as a keeper of the past, in all its forms. A cupboard for both the world's history and its own.

I approached the ramp drawn on my map. It led to a smaller tunnel with a much lower ceiling. Overhead, a yellowed sign said simply LUXOR in an archaic script. Twenty feet farther on, the narrow tunnel ended, walled off to frame a blue door. I went through it, not knowing I would wind up in Egypt.

I know where it is!" Hebe barked as he raced out of the room. Helen's eyes followed him with a sideward glance as she sat down in a wicker chair. A stream of desert light made her incandescent.

My dark, modern clothes poked vividly into the diffuse atmosphere and sand-colored palette. I felt like a fly on a projection screen: too dark, too saturated.

"Last week we went down the Nile and visited this temple," Helen said, making polite conversation in her singsong voice. "Hebe!" she yelled to the other room, "What was that temple called?"

"Dendur."

"Dendur, yes Dendur. That's it. Roman period. Built under Augustus. Ten BC, I think. Anyway, my brother, Bobby, was visiting, and he carved a name on the temple like some Grand Tour graffiti. Hebe was *furious!* 'Leonardo,' Bobby wrote. For fun he added 1820 instead of 1920! Such a hoot!"

She threw up her hands and rolled her eyes to the ceiling—a gesture of genuine hoot confirmation.

"You'll take the aqueducts back?" she said, abruptly changing the subject.

"The what?" They were only the third and fourth words I had uttered since arriving.

"The aqueducts," she said, "The tunnels below the museum where the water used to travel from the old Croton Reservoir down on 42nd Street."

"Right. Yes. That's how I got here," I replied. "I think. Susan in Mr. Trachner's office gave me a map and told me to look for the blue door. Somehow, I wound up here, in the desert. You said it's 1920 here?"

"Yes, this is Metropolitan House in Luxor; the site of the ancient city of Thebes. It can be confusing the first time, but the direct link with the 'home office' makes *everything* easier."

Helen waited for a sign that I was following her, but then just moved on. "This is the main base for the Met's Egyptian Expedition. Glorious, isn't it?! We come every dig season, October through June. It's been going since J. P. Morgan first sponsored us in '06. Hebe runs things and I'm part of the Graphic Section, mainly documenting everything in watercolor."

I knew the Met's Egyptian Expedition went on for thirty years, lasting until 1936, but I didn't know they kept it in the basement. Trachner had sent me to a pocket of space and time lost to the world, but preserved by the Met.

Again, I watched and listened.

Helen looked around and smiled, paused, and shifted abruptly again. "Good!" She clapped her hands on her knees and stood up. "Well, we're just delighted you came. It's a real *plum* of a favor!" she warbled.

"Found it," Hebe reported as he came back in through the doorway. He was using a broad, flat paint brush to softly sweep what appeared to be a flat stick lying in his open hand.

"Here you go," he said to me as he gave me what rested in his palm. "A four-thousand-year-old leg of lamb! Belongs to the Offering Bearer we found in the Tomb of Meketre. She's holding a whole basket full of meat. Somehow this leg got left behind."

In my right hand I held a nine-inch piece of painted wood, carved into the form of a sinuous animal leg, terminating in a pointed hoof that looked as elegant as a ballet dancer's foot. The painted leg was worn and chipped like an old, beloved toy, but the crimson color was still saturated and fresh, a simplified rendering of raw flesh. Above the hoof, a patch of white with black spots spread upward like a sock, a graphic glimpse of the animal's pre-butchered state.

I realized in that moment that Hebe and I were relay racers, passing a baton across time: 2000 BC, 1920, 1995.

"Didn't we find out that it's actually too long to be a leg of lamb?" Helen chimed in.

She turned to me and added, "We went to the butcher on market day and showed it to him. He said it was antelope or deer—or some sort of venison."

"Oh, I know, I know." Hebe muttered, "But leg of lamb is just better shorthand. No one says 'leg of antelope,' do they?" He looked at me as if expecting an answer, then kept going. "Ah that Meketre sure lived the good life. He had *tremendous* power in the Middle Kingdom. Known in inscriptions simply as 'Sealer.' Who wouldn't want to be a 'Sealer,' huh?"

I thought of Dick Trachner, perhaps the modern-day version of a "Sealer" with his discreet manipulation.

"So…," my voice trailed off, signaling my continued confusion, coupled with the persistent awareness that this test must have a final goal.

"Oh, it would be just ducky if you could bring the leg up to the Egyptian Department so they can put it in the statue's basket," Hebe instructed casually. "Tell 'em Hebe Winlock sent it. They'll know. That statue was a real star of the Meketre horde. One of a pair of goddesses. The Egyptian government got the one carrying the beer—they always get half of what we find.

"Ours is almost three feet tall, dressed to the nines in feathers and balancing the basket on her head with such humanity…"

He looked wistful at the thought of the four-thousand-year-old Egyptian woman, as if she were a former lover, then snapped from his reverie and blurted, "Splendid! Good to have that done. Back to the trenches now. Well, quite literally for you. You'll take the aqueducts back?"

"Uh, yes, sir," I replied.

"Splendid!" he repeated, "Always the best way. Lovely to meet you. I'd shake your hand, but we don't want to lose that meat again!" He winked, grabbed the hat marked WINLOCK, and left the room again.

I took one last look out the window to the boundless desert and its dazzling light. What seemed like a thousand workers crawled over the sand dunes like ants in a bustling colony.

But I couldn't linger. Like them, I had work to do.

I went back through the blue door, into the narrow tunnel, and down the dark ramp again. I found one of the staircases from the tunnels to the basement and emerged at the ground-floor Command Center with the small, wooden animal leg in my hand.

I borrowed a piece of paper and a cheese, wrote MEKETRE on the paper, and carefully wrapped it around the artifact, at once so ordinary and so incomprehensible. I scribbled "Egyptian Department" on the Recipient line of the yellow envelope and hand-delivered it.

"Dorothea is going to want to see this *immediately*," I told the receptionist in the Egyptian offices to encourage her to get it to the department's chief curator. The receptionist seemed unmoved. "Like, *now*," I added.

Dick Trachner's peculiar test seemed small and petty next to my dismembered antelope, but I still wanted to prove myself, still wanted to show that I could be that get-it-done girl. I decided to play it cool and go back to my stool as I would after any assignment, unfazed by the desert diversion.

Before I returned to the Development Office, I stopped at the Temple of Dendur in the Egyptian galleries. I scanned its surfaces and there, below the hieroglyphs, "Leonardo 1820" was carved with all the splatter and wit of any graffiti—the tender amusement of another age, Helen's brother, Bobby, having a hoot.

Next, I visited the galleries devoted to the Meketre treasure to see the Egyptian Offering Bearer. Her feathered dress and elaborate ankle bracelets mirrored my own sartorial ambitions. She rested on block-like bare feet, one advancing in front of the other, her gentle curves beautifully conforming to the shape of her unhurried stride—so different from my own pressured pace.

The serene expression on the Offering Bearer's face enhanced her enduring calm and seemed the ideal welcome to the afterlife. Her hand barely touched her square basket, balanced on her head and generously filled with meats of all kinds. Instead, the hand soared upward in a slim silhouette that emphasized her grace.

I noticed my own tense hands. It would be a while before I matured into any kind of elegance.

But right then, right there, in that gallery, I looked straight into the black ink of the Offering Bearer's eyes, and we met across millennia. Past and present leaned lazily against each other again.

She delivered meats.

I delivered cheeses.

GIFT MAN

The collection is monumental, peerless, transformative: The Met deploys every possible adjective to describe its importance and its magnitude. The fifty-four paintings in this one private collection capture a critical movement in art history: its early experiments, lost works, not always the biggest and boldest examples, but the most important, the most indicative of its core.

As paintings conservators, we are invited to visit the collection. Our swoons bounce within the quilted silence of its Park Avenue home. "Pristine condition," we whisper and sigh. We know these paintings could fill the very spot where the Met's holdings have a gaping hole.

The man behind this extraordinary collection—the Gift Man—is giving it all away. He toys with every eligible museum—Boston, Philadelphia, Washington, L.A.—before deciding who should receive his art. The spry seventy-year-old deftly allows rumors to swirl about private meetings and stealth negotiations, leaving each suitor desperate and grasping. Every museum is on its knees, box open, ring glinting, quoting Byron, Browning, Billy Joel—anything to make this romance rain.

The Met plays the game with gusto and skill: 85 percent of our collection has come to the museum by gift. We want these paintings. We want them with an itchy, greedy, determined kind of desire. Like a kid on Christmas Eve wants a puppy with a bright red bow around its neck. But it's bigger than that, because there's more at stake. More ego, more conquest. There's only one puppy, and only one museum will find it under their tree.

The Gift Man's publicist drafts press releases about each possibility so that he can consider how they read.

"A gift to the nation" has a nice ring. "A shocking sur-prise" also seems like fun. Ultimately, "strength to strength," the Met's favorite chestnut, wins.

We get the puppy.

A powerful magazine editor wants to mark the oc-casion with an image of the Gift Man at the mu-seum, surrounded by some of the masterpieces that he will now share with the world. The magazine's most famous photographer will take the picture.

The Famous Photographer's squadrons land in the Met's galleries like so many pigeons upon a ledge. They scout locations, remove unsightly details from view, adjust clouds to diffuse the light. There are test shots and trials and awkward discussions about how unusable the museum is as a backdrop for their work. "Not ugly," they explain, "just not workable for us. We really need to be somewhere with *texture*. Where would that be?"

They dismiss the Roman Court as "so beige" and the Met's original façade, still visible in the Petrie Sculpture Court, as "too brick-y." They speak constantly and cryptically of a journey: "The African Galleries are nice, but we need to take the viewer on a *journey.*"

"How 'bout Africa?" a guard murmurs in response to their marshmallow drama.

They seem to assume that the museum is withholding a secret set of rooms. And they are right.

We hide the conservation studios, siblings divided by medium: paintings, textiles, objects, paper, photographs, costume, arms and armor. The most beautiful among the sisters is ours, Paintings Conservation. Walls of twenty-foot-high windows fill the cavernous space with northern light. A forest of paintings crowds the room, propped on easels and against walls. Barbizon landscapes, German altarpieces, American portraits, modern murals. No frames. Our most heroic paintings sit raw and exposed.

The studio atmosphere is solemn. We work silently pursuing tender treatments that make no sense to the uninitiated: consolidating, swabbing, ironing, rolling. We clean a monumental landscape with Q-tips and fill tiny losses on a Renaissance panel with a miniature clutch of eyelashes. We remove a nest of pen scribbles—the pictorial complaint of a bored student—from a Matisse.

Despite our fragile work, the Famous Photographer gets access to this inner sanctum. A prize for the Gift Man.

In a gallery of monumental Buddhas, we guide the Famous Photographer's team to our anonymous locked door. We climb two stories up an industrial staircase where a gray corridor leads them to our studio, glowing at the end of the hallway.

Disturbing our hush, the Famous Photographer's team declares the space "so authentic" and "perfect just as it is." Then, they request changes. Light meters and unwelcome curiosity poke into our intimate world. They measure as if planning to redecorate, move in.

They return the day of the photo shoot, hours before the Famous Photographer or the Gift Man, and set up on one end of our long room. We imagine their piles of equipment tipping the whole space on its side.

We are pulled from our work and brought into the foreign buzz of these fast-moving creatures. Four masterworks from the Gift Man's collection are arranged for the camera. Old-fashioned hand cranks clamp the pictures into place on seven-foot-high wooden easels. Wheels make the easels mobile but vulnerable to the team's frenetic movements.

Lights are organized and test shots taken, while the Famous Photographer judges from some unknown, off-site location. We watch, saucer-eyed, as one among the team, a fit Viking with long hair and facial scruff, plants his feet where the Gift Man will eventually stand. The Viking turns his eyes to the camera like an aspiring underwear model, narrowing them with shameless conceit.

We look on, dumbstruck by his lack of self-consciousness. Our lives are devoted to our absence—to the idea that no trace of ourselves should be left in our work. We have succeeded only if our interventions—new varnish, retouching, repairs—are not just invisible, but reversible, able to be completely erased—wiped away—by future generations.

The Famous Photographer arrives hours later, good-humored and ready. Her team swirls around her, enthusing about the light and the exclusive location. She plays the cool older mom, chatting amicably with us in a practiced style meant to be both friendly and aloof. She understands her star power and shows little care for the inconvenience she has caused.

But the Gift Man understands timing. He will not be denied his entrance. He arrives just late enough to ensure that we are all waiting for him and enters the studio to a ripple of applause. He is then positioned near his paintings, on the mark where the Viking preened.

The Famous Photographer cheers and hugs the Gift Man like this is the opportunity of a lifetime.

"Oh, Gift Man," she coos from behind the camera, "I've gotta tell you, there is nowhere else I can imagine being than in this room, at this moment, with you, and these paintings." She stresses the *you* over *these paintings*, stroking his ego in a way that she hopes will show up on film.

The Gift Man responds in his trademark vaude-villian style. "Hey lady, everyone here is in the same business: We make things look good." He grins with a winking, complicit smile.

"I know the drill," he continues, *"Shoulders back! Tits out!"*

As he shouts the words, he snaps into the pose of kings and generals. It is as if a wind machine has been switched on, pushing against his deflated cheeks and whipping his remaining strands of hair.

"Oh, you're such a pro, Gift Man," the Famous Photographer cajoles.

The Gift Man knows his tits line will warm up the room and send us all home with a story. And isn't that the goal of it all, really? Sending us home with a story about him. Not just here in this room, but out there, in the world, forever.

And oh, do we tell the tale of this day again and again—for years! It is birthday cake and lollipops every time. We make it bigger and louder with each repeating, embellishing it, inflating it—and the Gift Man—until it almost bursts.

The photo shoot is efficient, extended just long enough to make it seem complicated. The Gift Man and the Famous Photographer leave together to continue their banter, while we restore the studio to its serene state.

We settle back on our stools and return to our delicate work. But we are changed, and as we clean our paintings with gentle swirling motions, the same song plays in our heads.

Shoulders back, tits out, we think, over and over.

We rearrange ourselves, lifting our torsos upright as if strings pull us from our shoulders and the tops of our heads. Our necks reach forward and our backs arch slightly.

Shoulders back. Tits out.

We look at Sargent's Madame X stretching high above us as we tend to her varnish. Then to Prud'hon's Talleyrand and Manet's saluting matador, all nearby. They've heard the Gift Man, too, maybe that day, maybe long ago. Different gift men through the years, all the same.

Shoulders back, tits out.

It's the card they all play, persisting and posturing to send us home with their story.

Slowly, imperceptibly, we experiment. Our spines a little straighter, our chests pulled taut, we allow ourselves a flicker of ego, a raindrop of recognition. And for just a flash, a blink, we try on a little glory, and become a little less invisible, a little harder to wipe away.

Shoulders back, tits out.

NIGHT MOVES

On Thursday mornings during his first few months as a security guard, Henry Radish had breakfast at a local diner called Nectar with his sometime girl-friend and fellow guard, Maira. Maira seemed to like him less and less every day. She was soft and what his English mother would call "Jewish-looking," with pale skin and dark curls.

They were both part of a new generation of Metro-politan Museum guards slowly replacing the retiring ranks who for decades had come through an extended network in Bay Ridge, Brooklyn. A new requirement that all guards have college degrees had shifted the makeup of the nine-hundred-person force. The rule traded old-timers, thick and sturdy as corner bookies, for performance artists and playwrights, musicians and video game designers. Maira herself was an aspiring singer and former mime.

Radish was often intimidated by Maira's Upper-West-Side American confidence, but he was sent small life rafts of superiority when she mistakenly referred to something as "a mute point" or a "codundrum."

"Henry," she declared one morning after he had found a rent-controlled apartment, "You should wallow in your good fortune."

He smiled and clicked his tongue, a technique he had developed instead of correcting her: *Revel*, he thought, *revel in your good fortune*. If he was wearing his Met tie, he would look down and flip it under itself, a habit to avoid eye contact.

Tall and thin with a flop of dark hair and pale eyes, Radish was striking, though not quite handsome. He had been taught by his mother that being thin was a sign of refinement, and so developed a peculiar vanity to accompany his angular frame.

Radish stayed with Maira because he liked sex, and it was hard to find someone to have sex with you during the day. Maira shared his overnight shift and his physical appetites, so the relationship was convenient if not very inspiring. It probably peaked when she nakedly mimed pulling him toward her with a rope.

Once, at the start of their evening shift, he and Maira had squirreled themselves away in an Education Center supply closet for a quick session. They hadn't realized that the Musical Instruments Department was hosting a concert that night, and the closet they'd chosen was where the roses had been stored for the conductor.

Nina Beerbower, the department's punctilious administrator, was unflinching when she discovered them and reached over their fleshy tangle to grab the vase. "Dammit, those flowers had better not be ruined," she sputtered and moved on.

A memo was circulated the following day:

THE METROPOLITAN MUSEUM OF ART
INTERDEPARTMENTAL MEMORANDUM

TO: Richard M. Trachner, Senior Vice President,
Operations
FROM: Philip Peterson Little, Chairman, Department
of Musical Instruments
RE: Uris Closet

April 27, 1994

While preparing for our benefit concert last
evening, members of my department encountered
a naked couple engaged in the pursuit of carnal
knowledge in a closet of the Uris Conference
Room. Of course, we musicians are used to such
indiscretion and indeed applaud this display of
youthful enthusiasm, but if this usage is to be
encouraged, the closet doors should be equipped
with an inside lock to prevent interlopers from
being nonplussed, and staff users should be asked
to check the day sheet first for possible schedule
conflicts.

cc: Bruno Parker, Chief Security Officer

No repercussions followed, no identities were
shared. At the monthly operations briefing, Bruno
Parker made reference to "fraternization among colleagues," which stirred some nervous chuckles, but

he ended it quickly, only recommending that such activities be "taken off-campus."

Radish had heard about a senior staff member who had kept his mistress and his dog in one of the museum's art warehouses and wasn't fired when this setup was discovered. He suspected it was the same guy who deprived the American Wing of a kitchen because he needed to shower after he shagged his secretary at lunch. True or not, the stories of this stranger helped relax Radish's anxiety that his tenure at the museum would be short-lived.

In the weeks that followed, he kept his head down, arrived early at the Command Center to receive his nightly postings, and found himself "guarding" with a comical intensity that made him squint his eyes.

What's your favorite work of art?" Maira asked over breakfast one day, before immediately offering up hers. "I love those jasper lips in Egypt. They're so languorous, don't you think?" Radish at first thought she said *glamorous*, but then remembered who was speaking. It had become a game trying to sort out what she really meant in these moments, and this one stumped him.

"Henry. Henry?" Maira demanded. "Are you even *listening* to me?"

"Oh, sorry," he replied, scrambling. "I'm just considering the answer to your question. I don't know. It's bloody hard to choose from the whole museum, but let's see...," he hesitated. "Perhaps that Adam sculpture in the Blumenthal Patio. He's got a real magic."

"That's a snooze," Maira replied, disappointed. "He's so stiff and he looks a little gay with that apple."

"Well, darling, he is Adam, after all," Radish answered with deliberate perk. "The fruit accessory is prescribed by the actual story."

"It's just another example of the male-dominated halicarchy," she proclaimed with conviction. "This fetishizing of the heroic male nude. And don't call me darling."

Radish flipped his tie and spooned too many scrambled eggs into his mouth to prevent the obligation of responding.

"Have you ever felt like the objects are kind of, well, reaching out to you?" Radish asked after swallowing.

"What?" Maira answered.

"Like when you look at something in the museum, you feel something, well, beyond what you yourself would normally know?" he continued.

"For example?" Maira raised a skeptical eyebrow.

"Well, do you ever get cold near the *Washington Crossing the Delaware* painting? Or feel a breeze near that eighteenth-century Indian watercolor of the huge bat in the Islamic Galleries, like it's flapping its wings?" Radish smoothed his pants knowing that he wasn't getting any traction with Maira.

"No, Henry, I don't," she smirked, "And you sound like a fucking lunatic."

Radish didn't mention that he could also hear the complaints of the boys in Washington's boat as they crossed the Delaware: "This was a crap idea," the soldiers grumbled as Radish shivered.

"Right. Of course. It's just, well, they are great paintings, I suppose. Powerful stuff...," Radish stammered. He stood up and tucked his shirt into his pants for the third time since they'd sat down. "We should probably go," he said to end the conversation.

Radish remained distinctive among the guards for his tidiness. He never liked to be wrinkled. His museum uniform, made from a synthetic that could be run through a machine and still not show a crease, was kept with meticulous care. He was perhaps the only guard who grumbled that the Met's cleaning service, rather than truly pressing the shirts, simply left them stiff with starch.

Sometimes Radish would go up to the European Paintings galleries and admire the paper-like collars on the Dutch portraits. The people looked miserable, but they seemed to glow in the silvery reflection of their confining neck gear. Radish felt their piety like a too-tight skin when he looked at their rigid posture and tart lips.

What he had tried to explain to Maira at breakfast was his curious ability to transfer the sentiment of the Met's art to his own soul. He experienced these things not like the average curator or visitor, but as if they were happening to him.

And not just piety and cold weather. Radish felt the triumph of Tiepolo's towering Marius, as if *he* were the victorious Roman general. He endured the tragedy of David's *Death of Socrates* like *he* actually stood there, in the room, when the gulp of hemlock went down. He would nearly collapse—soporific, tranquilized— as he looked at the three slumbering figures sculpted atop Lorenzo Bartolini's *Demidoff Table*.

Before that morning, Radish had never tried to discuss this phenomenon, this appropriation of feeling; it was beyond his control and so fell among the many things that both frightened and sustained him: Maira, Manhattan…his mother.

But he did wonder. Could others hear Carpeaux's Ugolino moan as he deliberated which son to eat? Could they hear the crowds around the Assyrian Gates of Nineveh? The pious chants in the Medieval Hall?

Radish had discovered the Met a few years earlier on his initial visit to New York, a present from his American grandmother when he turned twenty-one. He climbed the steps of the museum for the first time, entered the Great Hall, and had the strange urge to go immediately to the second floor and stand before a late-nineteenth-century photograph of the Countess de Castiglione. In it, she turns a single eye to the camera as she looks through a small oval opening in a velvet frame she holds.

Radish had never seen this image, didn't know it existed, but the pull through the galleries was nonnegotiable, as if a small child were dragging him toward something shiny and loud.

"Welcome," the image echoed in his head as Radish felt the bored privilege of a spoiled, beautiful woman. He did not find the sensation jarring. Rather, it seemed a poignant tribute to the distant dreams he himself had occupied for much of his life. He thought of his toy soldiers, arranged carefully in his mother's garden when he was a child. He had spent hours mimicking tiny, desperate cries to voice the fear and peril he imagined any real soldier would feel.

Radish stood staring at the Countess in the photo, cloaked in the relief that comes from recognition, like hearing a familiar word in a foreign language.

It was the beginning of something.

Where are you posted?" Maira asked as they stood in the basement at the beginning of their shift.

"Greek and Roman, Medieval, then the American Wing, then Blumenthal."

"Awww sweet, you can hang out with your little friend Adam," Maira taunted.

Radish didn't ask where she was posted, but he wanted to know. His affection for Maira persisted in spite of her teasing, driven by carnal need, inexperience, or both.

"See you later," he said as he trailed down the gray hallway. A canopy of pipes and ducts sheltered the four-block-long warren of corridors, filled with empty crates and ancient workrooms where art was packed and pedestals built. Yellow signs declared, "Yield to Art in Transit."

Most of the staff had left by the time Radish arrived each night. His night shift meant that he missed the final 5:30 "sweep" of the day when the guards moved from the perimeter of the building through all 962 galleries to make sure they were empty. Maira saw it once and described the guards as "optipresent," dramatically appearing from every direction like an occupying army in the Great Hall.

From the basement, Radish would choose a staircase and ascend to the galleries, where he would push through one of many hidden doors into the radiance of what he thought of as "the big show." Often he chose to land near the Temple of Dendur, majestic against a wall of windows that allowed the ancient monument to collide with modern life and Central Park traffic.

Or he would select one of the original staircases from the museum's 1880 building, still hung with signs that read "TO THE GALLERIES" with gilded arrows pointing upward. From there he would arrive in the Medieval Hall with its glittering reliquaries overripe with faith and adoration; one held what was supposed to be Mary Magdalene's tooth embedded in rock crystal and surrounded by gold filigree, like a dental trophy for best extraction. Radish's gums throbbed violently when he looked at it.

Radish loved the instant when his slender silhouette stepped from behind the curtain, lit by the serenity of the museum at night. After the public had gone, there was an atmosphere within the galleries that took over like a thick fog. The silence crackled with a different energy, allowing the art to somehow relax, breathe.

That night, while Radish was in the Medieval Hall, he saw Maira through the colonnade leading to Arms and Armor and caught up with her.

"My brother used to love this stuff," she said to him as he approached. Her eyes swept across the room. "I guess every boy does, at some age."

Radish could hardly hear her. For him, the metal echoed with the howl of battles and death and smelled of burning corpses and ravaged flesh. At the same time, the ceremonial armor sang mightily, a parade of blind fervor bellowing around it like some overwrought opera.

"What?" Radish said too loudly, as if they were speaking at a rock concert. The word bounced around the room, pivoting off glass cases and stone walls.

"Why are you yelling?" she asked in a loud whisper, embarrassed despite their solitude.

"Sorry," he replied, again too loudly "Let's get out of here."

Radish pulled Maira into the Italian Decorative Arts Galleries where things were less turbulent for him.

"Where's your next post? I have a break, so I'll walk you there," Radish said gallantly, knowing that surveillance cameras watched their every move.

"I've got to go to L.A.W. now," Maira replied, referring to the modern wing. Radish looked nervous. Modern art was complicated: at times stolid in its formalist acrobatics and then swirling and tumbling with death and mortality in a way that was overwhelming. Rothko's *No. 13* painting could simply bang him off his feet. He had learned to avoid it.

"Good," he said, "let's go by the Leigh Bowery portrait. That might be my second favorite work of art, if you're still interested in my list."

"The giant potato man?" Maira screeched. "Reeee-aally? I mean, I love Lucian Freud, and it's a great painting, but there's certainly no beauty in a big, naked fat guy on a bench."

Radish frowned. He often sought out the poetic mass of Lucian Freud's naked portrait of Bowery. The six-foot canvas could barely contain the figure's bulk of raw flesh, seen from behind, leaning forward with a tired, lumbering consent. Radish loved the picture's sleepy heft and felt it like a lonely embrace.

"I don't know," he said, deflated, "it soothes me sometimes."

"Have you noticed that all your favorite works of art are naked men?" Maira quipped, smiling. "If I didn't sleep with you so often, I'd swear you were gay."

"Well, I'll just have to keep proving myself then," he smiled and nudged her gently.

He left Maira in the modern wing and headed upstairs for the last ten minutes of his break. In the wake of Maira's bite, he knew his insecurity could be recalibrated with Bronzino's sixteenth-century *Portrait of a Young Man*. Its direct stare and mild condescension filled Radish with renewed swagger, like a houseplant freshly watered.

He moved to his post in the American Wing where he discovered an 1828 miniature painting no bigger than the palm of his hand, depicting only the ethereal breasts of the artist—swollen, glowing pearls within a silkened nest—painted for her lover who had married someone else. The tiny masterpiece sent him spinning with her desire. Her jealous passion tightened the crotch of his pants and made him lightheaded in the small limits of an otherwise bland room filled with traditional portraits.

"What are you looking at?" Maira snuck behind him, peered into the case, and laughed. As he sheepishly turned away, she noticed the swelling silhouette at his crotch. "Jesus!" she yelled, "Do you have a boner?!"

In earlier days, Radish would have scuttled into a closet with Maira to finish what the picture had started, but instead he escaped to the boys in Washington's Revolutionary boat to cool things down. Maira followed, still laughing.

"Well, my friend, I think we just found your new favorite," she joked.

Radish would look back on that evening fondly after Maira had grown tired of him. Only three weeks later, the break-up unfolded with a clash between his youthful reticence and her dramatic pouting.

"Henry, maybe I don't want to have sex with a guy whose arms are skinnier than mine?" she whined. "My therapist says it's not healthy for my body image."

"Darling, your arms are lovely. Their size has never diminished my attraction to you." Radish replied, in his youthful scrambling—and with an unfortunate formality.

"Stop calling me that! What kind of guy in his twenties talks like that? Daahhhling—like you're in some old movie?"

Radish sputtered. "Darling" had always worked for his father. OK, he would be more straightforward, more American.

"Maybe I like your fat arms?" His voice climbed upward at the end of the question—and he immediately regretted the words—as he reached for her.

She pulled away violently. "Nice! So, my arms are fat? It's a mute point now anyway, Henry," she pressed, "It's over."

Moot, he corrected in his head, *it's a* moot *point. She really would have been better off as a mime*, he thought.

The nights were long without Maira, and Radish drooped like a puppy that lost its chew toy under the sofa. Maira asked to be moved to the day shift so he never saw her, except once from the bubble of the morning bus as she walked into the museum at 84th Street.

Radish whiled away some of his loneliness at his posting near the third-century-BC Etruscan chariot, enjoying the thunder of its racing glory. But most often, he would go visit the slumping woman in Corot's painting *The Letter* to feel the crushing heartbreak of a kindred spirit.

In Radish's lowest moments, he tried to lean on his vanity. He knew exactly where all the reflective surfaces were: glass doorways, cases for Japanese screens, large-scale photographs in the Menschel gallery, all gave a full-length view—while the Wrightsman period rooms offered repeated reflections. How eighteenth-century France flattered with its faint candlelight and smoky glass.

But this once-reliable meal still left him hungry.

In the Greek and Roman galleries, he compared his own taut frame to the idealized nudes. As the streetlights raked across the Greek rooms along Fifth Avenue, Radish would jump from one to the next, flexing and posing to emulate the posture of each figure.

The dance would continue in the Engelhard Court, where he jockeyed among the American sculptures. He would begin with the golden Diana of the Hunt, alight on one foot and poised with her bow, and end by dramatically collapsing into the pensive Hiawatha, seated with crossed calves as he stroked his chin in contemplation.

Cameras captured this dance in the Security Control Room, but Radish didn't care much anymore. Rumors had long tied him to the legendary closet romp, earning him a bold and mysterious reputation. Stories like that were unshakable, and their details were blurred and bloated every day over the cafeteria hot plates.

Dave, a thirty-three-year veteran guard with a gold tooth and the cool of a rap star stopped him one day in the Staff Cafeteria to tell him he was the talk of the Sentry Booth.

"You're a real badass, my friend." Dave whispered over the coffee cart early one morning. Radish looked around to find the intended target for this comment, but only saw a serene, Medieval Department curator quietly reading a book titled *Holy War, Martyrdom and Terror* over her oatmeal.

"Well, er, thank you," Radish responded.

"Keep up the moves, my friend, keep it up," Dave said as he smiled and walked away, past the angelic medievalist.

This brief camaraderie with another guard was oddly buoying, but he still missed Maira. Still suffered the dull stab of his first heartbreak. Still thought of his comment about her arms and felt it like a withering punch. Still wondered how he might get her back.

Radish's anchor was *Adam*, the marble Renaissance sculpture he had told Maira was his favorite.

"Hiya handsome," he would say to Adam each night as he stood in the Blumenthal Patio, a double-height relic of sixteenth-century Spanish architecture named after the donor who gave it to the museum in the 1940s.

Adam was different from the other works of art. Radish always felt the statue's desire, not so much for the apple, but for some other satisfaction. It felt like hunger, but the pull was more desperate.

The two—sculpture and security guard—shared a fundamental, central ache.

It was while staring at Adam's naked figure that the fragile bubble of a solution sprang from Radish's mind. He just had to make *his* arms bigger than *Maira's*! *Huge arms*, he thought. *Big, muscly arms*. Adam didn't quite have them, but Radish could. Flexing, manly, pumped-up, action-hero arms. He neglected to envision how these bloated arms would look on his attenuated shape— outsized water wings on a late-learning swimmer.

The simplicity of this revelation overwhelmed Radish. It shot through him with a jolt, and he found himself twitching to get started on this new plan. His eyes ricocheted back and forth as if the first step was hiding in the room, his feet skittering back and forth in search of a direction.

Push-ups, he thought, *push-ups*.

The urge to pursue this new idea was childishly singular, and thrilling in its novelty. But privacy was needed. Posing with statues was one thing, but full-on exercise in his pressed uniform was beyond what he could share with the cameras. Radish looked at the door to the service stairwell off the Blumenthal Patio, a workout room if ever there was one.

As he slid into the limited space, the heavy door closed behind him, encasing him in bright fluorescent light. He paused, scoping out the perfectly sized landing where he stood and reassuring himself that there were no cameras to capture his impending activity.

The stairs' wide handrail would serve as the ideal rack for his uniform, and with practiced expertise he rigorously folded the synthetic suit. His pants hung stiffly alongside the origami collapse of his jacket and starched shirt, with his tie still threaded through the buttoned-down collar.

Radish began his push-ups in this private chamber, plunging forward with greater and greater vigor as if there were a trophy at stake. Sweat appeared on his forehead, confirming the cleverness of his decision to remove his clothes.

An experiment with a one-armed push-up had disastrous results likely to materialize in some curious bruising, but Radish remained undeterred. He imagined the exercise immediately inflating his flaccid arms.

Maira would be his again.

After ten minutes, he felt an urgency from Adam, a panic that swelled and pressed against the stairwell door. He hesitated for a second, then ignored it, consumed with his new plan.

It wasn't the sound Radish noticed first, but the shadow. From his push-up position, he saw the dark shape of a head and shoulders stretch across the floor in front of him.

Radish lifted his eyes to see Bruno Parker's thick black shoes on the steps above the landing. At the sight of his supervisor, Radish sprang to his feet, an inadequate superhero ready for action, a skinny guard in underpants. The scramble that followed looked like he was wrestling with his own clothes: They were fighting back—and winning.

Everything was wrinkled.

Parker raised a single eyebrow, shook his head, and walked back up the stairs.

Through the closed door, Radish heard a loud, indiscernible noise as he fell to the floor with a crushing pain in his legs, unable to move. He felt agony from Adam and worried that something had happened to the sculpture. Radish's head lay on the landing, heavy with regret, as if detached from his body. He suddenly thought of Maira; surely this would qualify as a "condundrum."

Radish longed to stuff the shirt smoothly back into his trousers, to pretend that what had been seen was not there and what he felt was just part of a dream. His night moves had been stilled, and reality—with all its creases and folds and heartless limitations—now painfully descended on him.

It was the end of something. The brokenness of everything.

MEZZ GIRLS

They were known as Mezz Girls. Everyone swore that the young women of Development's mezzanine offices were indistinguishable, one from the next.

That night, before the party, they were being trained.

It was still the Age of Socialites, a post–Bonfire of the Vanities, pre-celebrity era. A pageant of rich women with hard hair and important jewelry. Black-tie meant gowns that rustled as they swept across the Great Hall. It was the sound of expense.

The guests were due to arrive in thirty minutes, so the Mezz Girls listened carefully as Winny Watson's instructions hummed and rolled like those of a ballet teacher.

"Arms parallel, palms to the sky, and turn," she said. "*Aaand* again. Arms parallel, palms to the sky, and turn."

Winny, a museum volunteer and former Mezz Girl herself, insisted on this awkward movement as a graceful way of directing people without pointing. The maneuver began with elbows clamped to the waist, forearms positioned as if preparing to receive a heavy box. The "turn" signaled a swing of the upper body, torso twisting in the desired direction.

The Mezz Girls followed along, exchanging skeptical glances.

"What the fuck?" one snorted. The Mezz Girls liked to swear, but only amongst themselves.

Winny continued to issue instructions in her Park Avenue caw, wearing a one-shouldered gown that revealed ripples of loose flesh over her fit tennis arms. While her authority over matters like pointing had questionable origins, her Mayflower pedigree did not. She descended from Eatons on her mother's side and Fullers on her father's, creating a gene pool as shallow as a serving of consommé at the Colony Club—with a worldview to match.

The Mezz Girls were all pleased when the first tottering guest appeared in the Met's doorway, abruptly halting the lesson.

"Thank fucking God," they sang in unison.

When the partygoers entered the museum that evening, a miniature graveyard greeted them: a long table spread with hundreds of perfectly spaced envelopes the size of business cards, alphabetically arranged—one for each guest—and set atop a dark linen tablecloth. The pristine white rectangles rested on their half-opened flaps, a name carefully calligraphed on the front and a table number tucked within. It looked like Arlington National Cemetery for mice.

The curious sight of this tabletop graveyard was coupled with a ritual. The well-dressed Mezz Girls snapped up the correct card for each person entering the museum, efficiently—though not hurriedly—presenting it to them: "Good evening, Mrs. Astor. May I give you your seating card?"

As the rush of arrivals quickened, the swinging rhythm of card retrieval and distribution accelerated, growing almost competitive among the jostling Mezz Girls, with the ultimate goal of clearing the table. When an unknown guest had to retrieve their own card, the shortfall crushed the young women. Success meant the obliteration of the entire cemetery—a resurrection of sorts—as each guest thwarted the fate of the miniature tombstone. But some cards inevitably remained until the end of the evening. Sullen memento mori to those who never arrived.

I'm *bored*. This is *boring*. Are you bored?" They all heard Mrs. Leonard Havering address this question to no one in particular. Her defining impatience had amplified with old age, a slow lacquering built with fine layers of loneliness. She had just entered the Great Hall and was anxiously scanning the room as if searching for a missing cat.

"Oh dear, you know these evenings take a bit of time to pick up steam," the wise Mrs. Wilmington counseled after catching the remark. She delivered her comments as if waving away a slow, buzzing fly. "I hear the auction is unrivaled this year, so sip some champagne and get your bidding arm ready."

All this came from Mrs. Wilmington's mouth while she continued to move right past Mrs. Havering to avoid the risk of an actual conversation. Had Mrs. Wilmington simply flown away, it would have had equal effect.

The preppy wife of one of the museum's Trustees charged toward Mrs. Havering like an overgrown Girl Scout. Mrs. Towey never appeared quite right in a gown; even at the age of sixty-seven she looked like a star field hockey player on awards night, hair clipped with a single barrette at her temple, constantly adjusting the long strap of her evening bag like it was a backpack filled with books.

She cartoonishly kissed her own palm and then pushed her hand on Mrs. Havering's cheek with an exaggerated shove. The slap-kiss. It was her trademark. Mrs. Havering bristled, but the Mezz Girls enjoyed Mrs. Towey's unfiltered energy.

"Great to see you!" Mrs. Towey barked. "Another show here at the rodeo! Ha! Great! Bye!" She tackled her next victim before Mrs. Havering could even respond.

Everyone seemed to be moving but Mrs. Havering. She had somehow stranded herself on a rock as the social stream whirled around her. Her eyes skipped around the room, and she absentmindedly touched her hand to her chest and felt for the lavish sapphire necklace that spread across her gown. It reminded her of her wealth, quietly clarifying that she belonged in this crowd so clearly repelled by her presence.

In these moments, the Mezz Girls could tell that Mrs. Havering missed her late husband. They missed him, too. Leonard was the fun one, the gregarious foil to her hard edge. Over the years, his cupcake optimism grew into a glittery persona, drawing everyone into his jolly parade of banter and delight. "I'm just glad you're playing for our team!" he would cheer to the Mezz Girls as they took his coat or gave him his seating. "You'll be running this place soon!" They loved his attention, his bold trespass across the usual silence, if only for its recognition that they actually mattered in some small way.

M rs. Havering!" Lindie Garrison approached the small, smirking woman with a waving enthusiasm that betrayed her ambition.

The Mezz Girls knew that Lindie's infamy sprouted last year when she held a dinner party for thirty people and the waiters left midway through the meal. In her careful instructions to the caterer, she had neglected to sign the overtime clause. When the chef took too long preparing the halibut au gratin, the staff simply walked out at the hour they had been told.

The dinner party ended with a wine-soaked Mr. Garrison earnestly singing "Blowin' in the Wind" to their guests as he sat on the edge of the couple's bed with his acoustic guitar.

It would be a limping return for young Lindie.

"Lindie," Mrs. Havering replied with a neutrality that Lindie read as progress. "I would love to catch up, but I see someone from the Greek and Roman Department whom I must speak to about a sarcophagus."

At that very moment, a rose fell from one of the oversized floral arrangements in the four niches of the Great Hall; Lindie saw it and pouted, perhaps recognizing the possibility of a similar fate for herself.

One of the Mezz Girls also noticed the fallen flower and retrieved it with a swift, boomerang movement, scooping up the wayward rose and returning to her post like a ball girl on a tennis court. The Development Office trained its own like ninja. A Mezz Girl could sail across a room, airborne, to retrieve a dropped fork before it hit the ground. Legend had it that one of their ranks supported a broken elevator from below—a high-heeled Atlas to the elevator's sky—when the Emperor of Japan was briefly trapped inside.

Met style—a cocktail of European elegance and Protestant restraint—had rules, imperatives that defined every element of an evening, from the personalized seating distribution to the silent commandeering of a chair for an elderly Trustee, complete with a museum curator to keep her company. A stray, dead flower would not do.

Cocktails continued in the Great Hall, as furred and feathered couples gathered around the Information Desk, now transformed into a circular bar with waiters serving from within its perimeter. The lights were dimmed, and hundreds of votive candles spread across the steps of the grand staircase, conjuring a private night sky for the great and the good who now populated the Hall's cavernous space: men and women, middle-aged and older, puffed with the sort of lucky birth or financial achievement that inevitably led to big rooms filled with small chairs fashioned from gilded bamboo. The Met had convened its club, and this benefit to raise money for building the collection felt like its annual dance.

When Mrs. Wrightsman passed through the entrance, it was as if the Mezz Girls heard a dog whistle. They reflexively locked their eyes on her and smoothed their dresses. The collector of all collectors, donor of all donors, queen of all queens. Like royalty, Mrs.

Wrightsman didn't need attention, rather, she was to be protected from it.

The Mezz Girls watched with the restraint of a silent army as Met Director Michel Larousse bounded to the door for the museum's most important Trustee. She spoke in a porcelain voice that matched her fragile silhouette and went straight to business.

"Michel, I walked in with Danny Swillbinger and encouraged him about giving his collection," she said confidentially about the well-known collector of Fragonard drawings.

She then paused and added with a sly humor, "Just so you know I'm still pushing the firm."

"Indeed, you're our own prized pit bull," Michel smiled as he lightly took hold of her arm. He swam in her attention, relieved by her presence. It meant he could neglect everyone else.

A gong rang through the Great Hall. Again, the Mezz Girls snapped into action, springing from one troupe to the next to ask politely that they move in to dinner. Daphne, a Development veteran, approached a group near the Roman Galleries with a mild but deliberate force.

"Excuse me. If you could proceed to the Temple of Dendur for dinner now..." She tried Winny's patented upper-body shift to point in the direction of the Egyptian Wing, but felt like a Barbie with back problems.

Mrs. Randolph ignored Daphne's instructions, turned to her, and asked in her syrupy drawl, "Well what do *you* think, young lady? Who's the better artist, Picasso or Braque? Jim here thinks ol' Pablo was just a better salesman."

Daphne hesitated, rattled by the interaction, but then responded earnestly, "Isn't the most interesting period for both artists the moment when you can't tell their work apart? When they are side by side developing Cubism, and the work is indistinguishable?"

Mrs. Randolph raised an eyebrow and paused as Daphne panicked that she had overstepped. "I like you!" Mrs. Randolph replied brightly. "You're smart, and you're *decorative*." She appraised Daphne in her blue dress, then picked at it approvingly as if she were re-moving lint.

The ancient Temple of Dendur sat like a night-club on the Nile, dazzling and radiant in the slippery reflections of the water that surrounded it. On the platform around the Temple, thirty-two tables ached under piles of flowers, porcelain, glass, and silverware. A piano sent an endless song into the air.

One of the Mezz Girls, who had trained as an archaeologist, wondered what anyone would make of a society represented by such mass-produced excess, a society with ritual public sacrifices in the form of fundraising auctions. She looked down at the pamphlet that sat at each place. She had heard about this year's special packages, designed to encourage the men to bid.

Many of the Mezz Girls were in the meeting when Mrs. Barnley, the evening's formidable Chairwoman, declared that "men are the new women" for any successful charity auction. The evening's offerings seemed to represent her best guess at what that meant.

THE METROPOLITAN MUSEUM OF ART
ACQUISITIONS BENEFIT AUCTION

October 4, 1999

The Lance-a-Lot Package
Grab a weapon and suit up in full armor for a Central
Park joust that everyone will enjoy. All equipment
courtesy of the Arms & Armor Department.
Commemorative video included.

Guns!
Horses not your thing? There are other Arms to
explore. How about a few rounds in the Museum's
basement shooting range? You can keep the paper
targets and brag about your blow holes.

Die Like an Egyptian
Jar up Uncle Miltie's favorite snacks and send
him smiling into the afterlife. The Egyptian
Department technicians know all the ancient secrets
of preservation. Let them deliver what no modern
funeral can with the ultimate in personal care.

Row, Row, Row Your Boat
Whip by those other boats in the Central Park lake
with a canoe from the African Galleries. It's all the
adventure of world travel, right here in our backyard.

The Mezz Girls watched Mrs. Havering approach
her table, scowling. They also noticed the strange man

with elaborate facial hair who stood next to her seat as if waiting for her. He had a thick gray beard along the sides of his face and a walrus-like mustache, with what appeared to be a two-inch wide landing strip shaved up his neck to his lower lip. It made his chin look like a tiny, naked ass bending over to expose itself beneath a hairy dress.

"Look who's here, ladies," one of the Mezz Girls said, "Everyone's favorite asshole." They were used to the ghost of Jacob Rogers showing up at these events to taunt and tease the guests.

"Old Havering's gonna meet her match tonight," Daphne responded, her eyes fixed on Rogers.

All the Mezz Girls knew Rogers. The locomotive magnate had been kicking around the Met since he died in 1901. Back then, he shocked the museum by leaving it his entire fortune. The six-million-dollar gift was a lottery boon, and the museum went shopping. Van Goghs and Bruegels and Greek vases, masterpieces by the thousand. The Met was still spending it.

But Rogers was also a legendary jerk, called "a pure animal man" in his own obituary. He often showed up at the museum's black-tie dinners like an embarrassing uncle at Thanksgiving. And as with any family, all the Mezz Girls could do was try to limit the damage.

I don't like anyone I don't know," Mrs. Havering cracked by way of introduction as she sat down.

"Indeed," Rogers replied with admirable gentility and a hint of agreement, as he instinctively pulled out her chair.

"I've lived too long and done too much to have to spend an evening with some stranger," she continued, now shouting upward as he remained standing.

Rogers's thick wool dinner jacket looked like a dusty theater costume, and she inspected it with a questioning glare. She also noticed the shifting quality of his presence, at once overwhelming and not quite there, and attributed its elusive character to the dramatic lighting that had been designed for the evening. Spotlights shot asymmetrically across the room, striping the Temple in their path and pooling in bright circles upon the gallery floor.

"I could not agree more, madam." Rogers's curt accommodation merely fueled her rage.

"I tell you, a single woman in this town gets treated like the help. I get shoved with any nobody they can find."

Rogers was unflinching; Mrs. Havering had indeed met her match. "No more than an unattached gentleman, I assure you. We have solidarity in that."

Mrs. Havering smirked and started her cat search again, rolling her eyes around the room with skittish speed.

"Why do I even bother coming to these things," she grumbled. The list of auction items lay on her plate, and she reviewed it with her lips tightened in tense disapproval.

"This place has lost all its dignity," she muttered—again, with no intended audience.

The Mezz Girls wondered if Mrs. Havering couldn't benefit from a joust or a few rounds in that firing range. Wealth could be a burden in New York if you joined the wrong game: So many rituals were required to distribute your money and stay relevant. But jumping on a horse and poking the innards out of someone at full speed, or shredding a target with a violent spray of well-shot ammo....Ah, the release that might deliver for her pent-up anger and resentment.

Mrs. Havering didn't seem to notice that the rest of the guests at her table had arrived. Two fortunate no-shows bracketed her and Rogers, isolating them from the six guests on the other side of the table. The Mezz Girls wondered if they should find fillers, but knew it was a boulder of an assignment for even the most genteel diplomat.

"Fuck it," they decided. Mrs. Havering's table would be closely monitored instead.

Rogers and Mrs. Havering spent the first course of the meal in an epic silence, as she continued to sway back and forth, bobbing and weaving in her seat, sizing up the other tables to identify everyone else's more favorable placement. Even Lindie Garrison had been placed next to a curator from the Asian Department.

Sliced cucumbers held the first course's salmon mousse topped with caviar. Rogers scraped off the mousse to eat it, then lifted the cucumber pieces to his mouth, scooping them up awkwardly with his knife and fork. His knife slipped while conducting this odd operation and a large cucumber disk careened through the air. A Mezz Girl intercepted it with the stealth flash of an outstretched arm, just as it was about to peck at the back of an expansive helmet of hair. One small seed escaped, stuck in the net of hairsprayed tendrils, hanging tenuously like a spider from its web.

After the first course, the auction got underway, helmed by a Christie's auctioneer who knew almost everyone there. Rumor had it that he had drawings of every Upper East Side residence that might one day have property to sell—inventories and scribbled notes sketched on cocktail napkins in cramped powder rooms during dinner parties and receptions, tracking each home's future potential as a source of revenue.

He dove quickly into the first item, the Lance-a-Lot Package, which drew bids at a steady clip, easily reaching $750,000. The momentum slacked as the price neared one million. Unfazed, the auctioneer shifted gears and began to promote the package's commemorative video. He pointed to the flickering projections playing behind him on the wall: old black-and white films of museum staff dressed in armor from the collection as they jousted in Central Park.

"In the early years of the twentieth century, Trustee Edward Harkness used his Hollywood connections to get a movie camera for the Met's Egyptian Expedition," the auctioneer explained, "In the off-season, the camera returned to New York, and, as you can see, the staff got a little creative.

"This is once-in-a-lifetime stuff, people. Do I hear one million?" he added.

"*One hundred and twelve* million!" Rogers called out impatiently, with an old-fashioned stiffness that just narrowly veered from a British accent. With his formal intonation, he sounded like an overeager amateur on stage.

The Mezz Girls rolled their eyes.

"Now he's fucking with the auction," one of them hissed.

"I bet that amount is what his original gift would be worth now," another one added, shaking her head and folding her arms across her chest.

Mrs. Havering pivoted dramatically toward her neighbor. Her eyes widened with shock, as if she had finally found the cat she had been hunting for all night, only to discover that it had a hundred and twelve million dollars. Leaning back in his chair, Rogers moved into one of the streams of light and now seemed like a reflection in a cloudy mirror. She could have pushed her hand right through him.

Murmurs rippled through the stunned party, and the bewildered auctioneer dropped the hammer without so much as a countdown, anxious to lock in the bid.

"Sold for one hundred and twelve million dollars to the very generous gentlemen at table twenty-three!" he shouted.

Hesitant, confused applause broke out, and immediately a fuming Mezz Girl appeared at Rogers's shoulder, knowing that she had to keep up the charade of his antics.

"Your name, sir?" she asked politely, her pen poised above her clipboard.

The crowd hushed with a prying quiet—the leaning curiosity of the rich—interrupted only by the scrape of chairs turning toward the man's table, waiting for his response.

"Jacob S. Rogers," he proclaimed, then paused for effect, "of Rose Lawn, Paterson, New Jersey."

"Paterson, New Jersey??" Mrs. Havering exclaimed into the silence, now doubly slighted by being seated next to someone from New Jersey. *"No one is from Paterson, New Jersey!"*

Confusion gripped the room. Some had heard of Jacob Rogers and began to whisper questions in a real-time gossip chain. The chatter swelled and grew louder.

Enjoying the disorder, and the fury he had inspired among the Mezz Girls, Rogers stood up from his chair, stroked both sides of his substantial beard, and crossed the room. The guests quieted as they watched him move through the tables.

After descending the few stairs from the Temple platform, he walked straight through the gallery wall, dissolving into a cloud of shimmering dust. The Mezz Girls heard him snicker as he left.

"Bastard," they muttered.

The crowd exploded again with more questions.

"Typical!" Mrs. Havering howled from her perch, now fully exasperated. She craned her neck and scanned her table incredulously; the cat was lost again.

Then she twitched, and her face suddenly softened. She registered the strangeness of Rogers's appearance and disappearance: If Rogers was a ghost, then maybe her husband, Leonard, could be in the room, too?

Her eyebrows curved into gentle arches framing a new depth in her eyes. Her stern, pursed lips relaxed into an expression of hope and expectation. She brightened, sitting upright like a young woman in her gilded chair, as if waiting for someone to ask her to dance. She gazed around the room again, but this time breathless, her heart quickening with the idea that Leonard could be near.

When Leonard Havering rested his hand on his wife's shoulder, all of her indignation and anger fell away. She gasped and floated upward to him, relieved, renewed.

The Haverings swayed together within the commotion of the rustling crowd, a waltz of memory and comfort. A tent of light formed a cone of glittering dust just for them, as they moved within a bright circle upon the floor. Leonard glowed as Rogers had, ethereal and indefinably vague, while Mrs. Havering clutched the back of his dinner jacket with childlike fists, a desperate attempt to keep him.

"I don't like anyone I don't know," Mrs. Havering whispered, this time a confession rather than a complaint. She buried her head in Leonard's chest and finally spoke the truth, "I think you're the only person I've *ever* really known."

He smiled—that blooming, optimistic beam that always sliced through her despair—and pulled her closer. "I know," he soothed, his voice as clear as water, her face lifted to the past, "I know."

Over at Michel's table, Mrs. Wrightsman sat serenely, enchanted by the Haverings and the gentle chaos Rogers had stirred. In the raking light, she looked just like the Met's marble head of Athena, goddess of wisdom, from the late second century BC— bought with the Rogers Fund in 1912.

LOST

Morning sir," Walter said cheerfully, as he cleaned the front steps of the Met with a scoop and broom. "You early today, or am I late?"

Walter had begun to recognize Melvin over the past few days and sensed that something was off. In his usual way, he offered kindness rather than judgment. Neither a tourist nor a museum staff member, Melvin had the air of a weary local. He always sat near the top of the steps just to the right of the doors, where Walter would start to clean, working his way down to the sidewalk.

"You must be slacking," Melvin said, "I've been here for hours waiting for you to get started. And don't miss that sesame seed I just dropped."

Melvin smiled so Walter knew he was kidding. He wondered what it would be like to do a job with such direct and clear goals. Surely there weren't any politics in custodial work, only specific assignments and tasks: a day's work for a day's pay. Or were there arguments over shifts? Or who had to scrape up the old gum? Turf wars over the best broom?

"Well, I'd better speed things up then!" Walter replied, comically moving his own broom back and forth at a rapid speed.

Melvin laughed and went back to his bagel, tearing at it with his teeth as globs of wet cream cheese oozed from its sides and dropped weightily into a paper bag. He continued to eat it with raw, messy bites, leaning forward over his substantial girth to keep from staining his jacket and tie.

Three pigeons pecked at one of the fallen sesame seeds, their necks bobbing forcefully as they tried to retrieve it. After a minute, Melvin extended his leg to kick the stout gray birds. They flapped low to the ground, skirting along the stone like broken kites, only to return right back to the elusive seed. Melvin kept repeating this cycle, extending his leg and observing the persistence and stupidity of the pigeons as they returned.

"Are you harassing my staff?" Walter yelled from ten steps below. "They're union, you know."

"Well, they do seem to stick together," Melvin replied, almost admiringly. "You know, when they're done, they're gonna crap on my head."

M elvin had taken up residence on the Met's steps five days earlier, after getting laid off from his job. He felt both hidden and exposed atop the majestic heap.

In his gray suit, he maintained the uniform that had ferried him forward across twenty-two years of employment, starting with the first, sweatingly cheap version he had bought for his City College graduation in 1977.

His small head poked from his white shirt like an ancient turtle: a sloping chin leading up to a mouth unbalanced by the exaggerated overhang of his thin upper lip. Above, his flattened nose formed a puckered runway to his advancing forehead and the bald stretch of skin that ended in thick folds at the back of his neck.

It was still early, close to 7:30 AM, but he had to leave his apartment at the usual time to keep up appearances with his doorman. He could not yet envision a world in which his routines were fully unraveled. Until he could develop a new ritual as an unemployed, middle-aged man, the museum would serve as the shell to his snail, a glorious act of beauty concealing his slow, rubbery self.

Melvin propped his worn briefcase against his side. The swollen bag was closed with a large buckle, its leather surface scuffed and cracked with the ravages of a thousand subway rides. An insurance man always had paperwork, the accessory of his trade. Now the tired case was filled with blank sheets to maintain its heft when the doorman insisted on carrying it to the elevator at the end of the day—a service only provided in the few months before Christmas tips. Those empty pages made Melvin's stomach sink.

What passed for a doorman at Melvin's Third Avenue rental was the costume change of a janitor into a thick polyester coat with three bars on the shoulders—a man at the door rather than a doorman, with the same coat rotating among the building's meager staff, regardless of size or shape. But Melvin quietly knew, with an almost anthropological clarity, that those men were the only people who registered his existence each day.

"Hey," Melvin shouted to Walter, "What's your name?"

Walter ascended the stairs and nobly extended his hand. He was neat and compact in his carved musculature, and moved with a steady, deliberate pace that was confident and consoling.

"Walter," he said, "Walter Howe."

Melvin shook his hand. "Melvin. Melvin Bleckman." His old salesman instincts fired and then fizzled.

"Nice to meet you Melvin." Walter turned to go back to his work, but Melvin interrupted him.

"Hey Walter," he said, "Any idea why this building was never finished? What are those piles of stones up there supposed to be?"

Melvin looked upward to the four piles that sat above the columns on the façade, like some bored child had abandoned them. They were clearly meant to represent something other than unrefined pyramids of limestone.

"You know," Walter replied, proud to talk about his museum, "I asked someone that once, and they told me that the guy who designed this building wanted them to be sculptures representing different times in history. The first one was supposed to be ancient and the last one was supposed to be modern, but I don't remember the middle two. I guess the idea was that all the art inside could fit into one of those categories." He paused and looked up. "But they ran out of money and never got around to it."

"That happens," Melvin said grimly, now back to thinking about his own dilemma. Today was his appointment at the unemployment office, his first public admission that he had no job.

"Yes it does," Walter responded, "I kind of like them unfinished. It's nice to think of this old place as a work in progress."

Walter returned to his sweeping, and Melvin considered the idea of four categories that would hold everything in the Met. Life and death, to be sure. Sex, money…power…war…religion…love….He thought about grouping them into four sculptures. Life and death, sex and love, war and religion, money and power. Surely some artist could make four statues about all that.

Maybe it was this deliberation, or his trepidation about the unemployment office, but for whatever reason, that day, the inside of the museum beckoned to Melvin. He had been inside before—school trips to the Egyptian Wing, and an ill-fated date with a squat woman from the actuarial department—but not since his exile on the steps.

As Melvin waited for the Met to open to the public, he watched the looping activity on the museum's plaza: a food vendor scooping stagnant water from the oblong fountain for cooking his hot dogs, his curbside cart covered in American flags and labeled Disabled Veteran; mean girls in shrunken school uniforms with bare, coltish legs, gossiping and spitting gum onto the ground before entering the Marymount School across Fifth Avenue; a Wall Street banker stepping his expensive English shoe into one of the sticky, pink wads and pulling it along with him to the cab stand at 82nd Street; the awkward ending of a date that had started the night before: he, hungover and evasive, she, eager and overdressed; the strange proximity of two rats humping nearby, one mounted atop the other, aping the couple's unbridled fucking just hours earlier; excited tourists clocked to the wrong time zone, too early for the Met, but elated by the sight of genuine New York City rats; a bike messenger, spandexed like a superhero on a stripped bike mummified in duct tape, whipping down the avenue and then leaping over the curb to escape the path of a cab stopping to pick up the Wall Street banker; a homeless man dragging a tall wooden cross south toward the park entrance along with a cardboard sign that read, "He is comming. Are U ready?"; a goth high school student handing the homeless man a cigarette when asked if one could be spared, and then the careful acrobatics of balancing cross, sign, and cigarette simultaneously, a challenge never faced by Jesus; a Park Avenue matron clad in quilted jacket, Belgian loafers, and cauliflower hair, competing with her greyhound for minimum weight and maximum elegance; an elderly man, lumpen and stiff, clutching his walker and dragging himself forward as if toward Death itself; his nurse beside him, seeming to ignore the slow and incontinent subject of her toil; and Walter, his crisp silhouette outlined in the late September sun, carefully sweeping as if the plaza were his own front porch.

Life and death, sex and love, war and religion, power and money. *Not just in the Met,* Melvin thought to himself. *Right here on these steps.*

A t 9:30 the museum opened for the public, and Melvin clumsily unfolded himself from his perch, tossing his crumpled bagel bag and empty coffee cup into the trash bin to be the first through the doors. His appointment was at 12:30 so he had plenty of time.

The Great Hall welcomed him with its enormity and luster, like entering the inside of a colossal diamond. Melvin was immediately struck by how the bright, light-filled interior offered him more anonymity than the steps. Under the towering domes he seemed even less exposed, happily inconsequential within this warehouse of so many different worlds.

Melvin's own apartment sat in a dim, sluggish light no matter what the time of day, the pallid flatness of its alley view giving way in the evening to the unchanging moon of his neighbor's kitchen light across the airshaft. His two rooms were sparsely furnished with a lumpy sofa, an old television, stale bed sheets, and a poster of a Warhol soup can that had been left hanging on the wall by the previous tenant.

None of this really mattered to Melvin, who went to his office seven days a week, the pretense of work disguising the time-filling comfort of his cubicle. In the seventeen years he had lived at 1577 Third Avenue, not a single guest had crossed his threshold. When he watched TV crime shows, he thought about how the dust of those rooms contained his own, lonely DNA, and no one else's.

He approached the admissions desk and pulled a dollar from his pocket, knowing that a donation of any amount could get you an entry button. He clipped the metal disk to his lapel, a vibrant turquoise against the drab suit, and felt like he had earned a merit badge. An unaccountable sense of belonging washed over him.

His plan was to move straight ahead toward the central staircase and push himself deep into the building, hoping to find some treasure to direct his journey. He crept along the north side of the staircase with faltering strides that seemed specifically choreographed for his short, thick legs and uneven posture, the briefcase serving as a ballast to his wobble.

A large mosaic fragment greeted him: a bejeweled woman with immense brown eyes, compassionate and knowing in their direct gaze. He passed the shining Byzantine chalices and elaborate gold accessories of early Christianity and stopped to look at a set of silver plates that illustrated the story of David like a comic strip. Battles with Goliath and a lion, described with flinging drapery and simplified expressions that made the hero resemble a middle-school doodle.

He then plodded past the candy-colored stained-glass windows and moved toward the monumental Spanish gate that divided the Medieval Hall. The

Hall itself was a cool cave at the building's center, like the lungs of a giant whale. The arches that punctuated its sides seemed to form a ribcage stretched wide to contain some ancient breath it had pulled in long ago and held steadily.

Melvin thought about the museum inhaling so much of the world—all that history, all that spiritual juice, all the passions and laments of each visitor—without ever really exhaling. He regarded the stone-clad walls as somehow porous, allowing the particles of time to soak needily into their surfaces.

How exhausting to hold everyone else's shit, he thought. He considered the acrid linoleum of his apartment's cabinets and floors, so resistant to absorption that everything clung to its surface, a sticky film across the impenetrable material of his life.

Beyond the Medieval Hall, through an arched opening aligned with the gates, an expansive gallery stretched between the French period rooms to the south and the English period rooms to the north. More polished objects filled the cases of this gallery, while tapestries cloaked the walls in a faded glory rooted more in bounty than belief.

Melvin found a bench to rest his office-conditioned body and the growing burden of his briefcase. He had been in motion for only twenty minutes but had already expended the daily dose of energy that he once used at work for his repeated laps to and from the coffee machine.

He slouched forward to consider his next direction, facing France as though he might enter and buy a baguette.

A bold brightness drew him to look to his right, where a skylighted space glowed like a sunrise on the horizon. Melvin stood up to poke his head in, leaving his heavy briefcase propped against the bench.

He crossed the threshold of the space to find no art in sight. An enormous, open area expanded to create an angled shape—a baseball field appendage hanging into Central Park from one of the museum's original façades. Generous aisles allowed you to walk around the perimeter of a two-story open core, capped by a glass pyramid. Staircases with polished brass handrails gave access down to the lower floor.

Between the aisles and the central open area were unadorned walls, each pierced with enormous rectangular openings, like the ghosts of some long-lost series of murals. The gridded windows of the sky-light projected an enormous black web over the fields of white concrete.

This space was disorienting, and Melvin wondered if he had wandered into another museum, a place that no longer held the breath of centuries, but trapped a different kind of air: crisp, clear, new.

He noticed a guard approaching and was strangely relieved.

"Excuse me," Melvin said, "What is this place?"

"The Lehman Wing," the guard responded. "One guy's collection kept all together back here by itself. If you go through that opening over there you can see everything the way it was in his house."

The guard pointed toward a large, square portal along the perimeter of the space. "And man, those were some sweeeeeet digs." He smiled, a gold tooth glinting in the penetrating light.

"Jeez... wonder what he had to pay for this?" Melvin replied, arching his neck back as if he were measuring the cost per square molecule of air.

"Oh, that's some real dough, you know it," the guard shook his head in disbelief. "Not too many people come back here..."

"Well, thanks," Melvin replied. "I may as well check out his stuff." He spoke as if there were a tag sale inside.

The extreme arrogance of this monument fascinated Melvin, and he wondered how it had happened. How did one guy make a deal with the Met to get all this space with *his* name on it?

The privilege and strength of this complete stranger made Melvin's own paltry footprint in the world feel even more trivial, particularly now that he had lost the only traction he once possessed.

Melvin slipped through the unmarked opening that the guard had shown him and approached a glowing red room at odds with the bleached interiors of the vast open space. Inside, just as Robert Lehman had specified before he died in 1969, were the old red velvet curtains and flocked wallpaper from his family's lavish house on West 54th Street.

The room was small but filled with objects, its tall ceilings evocative of more stately proportions. Below the crimson wallpaper was a dado of deep brown wood against which Renaissance chairs and elaborately sculpted chests were placed. The whole space was outlined with intricate dark wood moldings along the ceiling, layered with swags and rows of ornament.

Over a marble fireplace, its surface encrusted with further extravagant decoration, hung El Greco's painting of St. Jerome—a wizened, bearded face, painted with gestural streaks, perched atop a voluminous red cloak, a portrait of intensity and disproportion. St. Jerome was flanked on the left by another El Greco, *Christ Carrying the Cross*—serene with glistening eyes despite the weight of his burden, a tragedy foretold by the painting's brooding skies.

"You should try that with a cigarette," Melvin murmured to himself.

On the right was a roughly painted Rembrandt, a diminutive man with a broad hat and bright eyes set into a piggish face.

The opposite wall held a large Goya of a countess and her infant daughter—both glimmering in satin and lace—the mother staring away from the doll-like child. The countess appeared devoid of emotion, a stern porcelain mask within a dull haze of brown hair. Four eighteenth-century paintings of Venice, enlarged postcards of an unchanged city, surrounded the Goya portrait.

Melvin walked slowly around the room and read the labels on each work of art: life and death, sex and love, war and religion, power and money. Small, dark statues of satyrs and angels stood like cast shadows in a long case. A group of sixteenth-century Limoges enameled objects weighed upon old shelves behind glass.

A bronze sculpture of a woman sitting on top of a man down on all fours caught Melvin's eye, and he leaned in to discover that it was a late-fourteenth-century vessel illustrating a tale in which Aristotle allowed himself to be humiliated by a seductive woman named Phyllis in order to teach his student, Alexander the Great, a lesson. Sex and power, Melvin thought.

A pair of Dutch portraits depicted a bleak couple with bulbous bodies and dour prosperity. Power, but, Melvin suspected, probably not much sex.

Melvin could see other rooms beyond the red one. A compelling painting of a woman in a blue dress hung over a fireplace in the next gallery, and two sinuous brass chandeliers led the way to further velvet walls beyond. But he found himself happily trapped in the consoling womb of this first chamber.

In the center of the room, facing the fireplace, was an unremarkable old sofa, modest in scale, wide enough for only two people of Melvin's size. This was Mr. Lehman's real trick, the clever tactic that he knew would allow visitors to truly understand what it was like to live with masterpieces—to sit and read the newspaper with Rembrandt, to do the crossword puzzle with El Greco.

Melvin hesitated, then sat on the old sofa, rigid and erect, expecting a guard to enter to correct him. But there was only silence. He looked like a patient in a dentist's office, waiting for what he knew would be a painful appointment.

His eyes swirled around the sumptuous room, searching for a way to comprehend its luxury. He felt the chasm between this privileged world and the lonely nights he spent with a TV tray and sitcoms for company. Maybe an occasional evening of porn.

An image of the plastic-covered furniture from his childhood living room flashed in his mind.

Melvin's posture slackened into its usual weak arc. He sank into the sofa—really not that different from the old couch in his own bland apartment.

Eventually—out of torpor, allure, or both—the Lehman sofa's cocooning depths consumed him; he loosened his tie and slid down into the cushions, a gesture of comfort and occupation.

Sitting within this grandeur, Melvin realized the frailty of the categories he had devised on the steps. What he had forgotten was something much bigger than those themes of love and death and power. What he encountered now was overwhelming beauty. It dominated his senses. It was a foreign experience, but he didn't need to be rich to recognize it.

The combination of the soft patterned walls, the gilt curves of the frames, the subtle surfaces of the paintings, the warmth of the bronze statues and luminous wood—it all overtook him.

Melvin's much more ordinary pulp and flesh literally dissolved into the room, unable to sustain its existence against the might of such splendor. The more beauty he absorbed, the more it absorbed him.

An equal transfer, melting his common self into Mr. Lehman's illusion.

What began as a dip into another man's world became a slow vanishing. Melvin's quotidian flab, his manufactured wool suit, the eroded leather and rubber soles of his shoes, all dissipated, followed by his turtle head, drifts of dandruff, meaty hands, and swollen, hairless ankles. It all quietly disappeared into soft, twinkling flecks.

Melvin observed his own dissolution with relief. The yoke of decisions and bills and his unknown future loosened and then, finally, released. There would be no meeting at the unemployment office, no admission that he had lost his job.

For hours he sat there, until he was completely invisible. His once grainy figure on the gallery video cameras faded like a thin cloud burned away by the sun.

All clear! No one's in here," a guard shouted as she walked through the room at about 12:30 PM.

As she passed, the newly invisible Melvin remained tucked into Mr. Lehman's sofa, staring at the paintings of Christ, St. Jerome, and the piggish man: his new roommates. They were a humorless bunch—more pathos than party—their oversized hands occupied with books and a cross. But still, the total number of Melvin's friends had just tripled. That was surely something. Of course, people at the office had called him Mel and asked about his day, but that was an office farce that adults were taught to mimic. No one had contacted him since he was laid off.

"I'm not that fun either," Melvin confessed to the threesome, by way of introduction.

Melvin kept his back turned to the Goya countess and avoided the pouting Dutch couple, knowing that he would conquer them with the infinite time that lay ahead. Satyrs, angels, an enameled Mars and Minerva, were all by his side. That saucy Phyllis could ride him anytime.

Melvin had claimed his future, his new home—a fresh routine among masterpieces and the lush trappings of a Lehman life. Life and death, sex and love, war and religion, power and money: all in this perfect room, its every surface coated in beauty.

Walter was surprised when he didn't see Melvin on the steps again. But he would think of him every time he looked up at those uncarved piles of stone.

No one else noticed Melvin's absence except his janitor-doormen—and only months later, when they were counting their holiday tips. Tommy, the youngest and most unreliable, said he'd heard Melvin had won the lottery, quit his job, and never come back. "Beautiful," the eldest, Gino, responded wistfully, not looking up from sorting his money, but immediately smitten by the fantasy. In that freshly hatched fairytale, Melvin became their Lehman, a presence they could visit and admire only now that he was gone.

ADAM

He was put on a pedestal long ago, centuries. He had decorated a Venetian tomb. Now a museum pedestal defined his world and gave importance to the cold, hard surface of his beauty. He was a relic of the Renaissance, all marble glow and graceful balance. A depiction of a naked, hungry Adam before he munched the apple.

This particular Adam was a favorite of scholars, but not of the visitors who crowded around other, more famous sculptures at the Met. His pure white form was the first life-sized nude of the Renaissance, idealized and simplified, with uninterrupted planes of muscle and a soft, dreamy grace. Supported by his right leg, his left foot lifted lightly off the ground, Adam was an art historian's work of art: garden sculpture to most, but revolutionary to those who understood his historical force.

So, Adam spent his days both admired and ignored. Through the centuries, his temptation to unhinge his glorious balance was as strong as that first apple must have been. He dreamt about bending his other knee or running his fingers through his hair. He imagined stretching the cavern of his mouth around the apple he held and hearing its hard crunch.

Over those many years, Adam observed everything from men in tights to women in bustles and, since arriving at the Met in 1936, modern, often messy museum visitors. The current batch strolled and yawned, stared at their phones and pulled their limbs in every direction. Adam had long sketched these movements delicately in his mind—the heel leads, the elbow only closes in one direction, the fingers fold inward—and felt a fierce pull for that same freedom.

Adam was five hundred and six years old when a guard called Radish arrived. Exceptionally tall and slender, he spent more time with the art than the others, and seemed to understand Adam's powerful craving for some kind of action.

Radish worked the night shift and would always visit the Blumenthal Patio where Adam stood. In the first few months, Radish shined: attentive and satisfied, occasionally joined by another, female guard. But later, he sulked: forlorn, always alone, somber and grieving.

Radish would stare at Adam and sigh heavily, a sound identically shaped to Adam's own yearning. The overlap forged a fierce connection between them—sculpture and security guard—both thwarted in their melancholy desire.

"Hiya handsome," Radish would say to Adam aloud, greeting him like an old friend. Adam hoped his distant expression, his glance upward and to the side, read as "don't I know it" in response to each of Radish's laments.

Adam longed to reach out to Radish, but he knew better. He did his time, held his pose, waited for his heroic turn. All the art at the Met could move, but not until it had to. Not until it was needed.

But he could start to plan. To prepare for that day, if it ever came.

He began by only moving at night, only in one direction, only slightly.

That first night, he put pressure on his left big toe and felt the pool of flesh expand. It was thrilling to stimulate that tiny piece of himself after five centuries.

Further experiments followed: a centimeter-long glide of the hips, a reverent dip of the chin, the quiver of a pinky—never more than that. A midnight flip of the wrist was overly ambitious and set him still again for days.

It was a Sunday night when Radish bubbled before him with a fresh enthusiasm. Adam observed this jolting excitement—this jumpy, skittish, twitching Radish—not understanding the source of his new-found gusto.

Radish then darted to the service stairs in the southeast corner of the gallery, flung the door open, and disappeared. But Adam could tell he remained just beyond the door. Shadows blinked through the gap below, and curious noises echoed from the stairwell into the gallery.

Moments after that heavy door closed, Security Chief Bruno Parker came through the Blumenthal Patio talking loudly into his two-way radio. "I'm in Blumenthal. I'll check the front door and Great Hall Balcony, then take the service stairs back down here. Meet you in the Medieval Hall in fifteen."

The radio clicked off as Parker left, and Adam knew his chance to move had arrived. He would save Radish from being found by his boss in that stairwell.

Adam's first, bold motion was like stretching after a cramped overnight flight. Rather than the isolated pivots of his earlier experiments, the heavy shift ripped through years of constraint. Arms and legs flexed, torso and neck twisted, hips propelled forward, even eyebrows bent into action as his toes and fingers curled.

His liberation flooded the room. Suddenly unbound, the thick exhilaration obscured everything. Space expanded within his body in a way that felt buoyant and rippled with life.

Then it happened.

He slipped. Or tripped.

And crashed.

The accident left him on the ground, reaching toward the door where Radish had gone. The security camera was not angled to capture the fall; the footage from an adjacent gallery would only reveal the sudden appearance of Adam's head on the floor.

His legs had shattered. Thousands of pieces, drifts of pulverized marble, numb and disconnected.

The pedestal had broken on Adam's way down, and Adam knew that it would be blamed, not him.

As he waited in the silence, he thought of the pedestal maker, a devoted carpenter who had served the museum for thirty-four years. The woodworker often visited his pedestals in the galleries with the humility of a farmer surveying a well-plowed field at the end of the day. This would crush him, too.

Bruno Parker never came back. Adam laid on the ground until Radish emerged, limping, from the stairwell and discovered him.

"Fuck," Adam heard him say. Radish paused, tilted his head to the side, and seemed to register what it felt like to be truly broken, scattered in a thousand pieces. He gulped, gurgling with a sound that cried for everything that had ever been lost. Then he turned and went briskly away for help.

They lifted Adam like a corpse, and he acquiesced quietly.

The flash of cameras accompanied the mourning curators, methodical conservators, and the museum's horrified Director. They could imagine no greater loss than the destruction of a work of art.

The gallery was treated like a crime scene. They carefully drew a grid over the floor, violently scattered with marble dust and shards. The contents of each square were gathered into a plastic bag and numbered, like art CSI.

It would take eleven years to rebuild Adam—along with a new stone pedestal. His pieces would reunite like gentle handshakes, miniature grips of silent, steady embrace.

Adam would become a star at the Met for his resurrection and be given his own gallery to match his new fame.

He would never move again.

And Radish would never return.

But Adam would always hold dear that electric memory of freedom, that sweet, syrupy, airborne moment of release. The rush of a boundary crossed, mixed with the black depth of the unknown. It seemed to last hours as he spun toward the ground that night, drowned in the whir and fizz of the gallery's darkness.

Now, Adam has fiberglass pins in his legs and invisible patches throughout his body. Like an ancient athlete, he has retreated. He no longer watches the visitors with intrigue and envy, no longer wonders when he will be needed. He lived that dream, tasted that apple, and now only tends to his stillness, and rests.

BIG-BONED

I like to pretend I'm judging the museum staff when they're paying for their food.

Sometimes I just raise an eyebrow at the amount as I type the individual prices into the cash register.

Sometimes I comment without any eye contact, out loud but as if I'm talking to myself, "Well, *somebody* is hungry today…"

They don't like this.

I do.

It's fun to get dramatic, and I exaggerate my Italian accent.

"Oh *bambino*, you be careful, right? It's winter now, but bikini season coming." I say this to the big guys in Construction.

You see, I'm "big-boned," like those Construction guys.

Man? Woman? Not sure.

I'm just a figure, an underdrawing.

In 1545, I was sketched in charcoal on a canvas by the Venetian painter Tintoretto. *Il Furioso*, they called him, because of his bold style and speed. He hoped my lines looked like Michelangelo's.

Michelangelo's drawing and Titian's color: that's all Tintoretto ever wanted for his art.

My hair is a series of thick squiggles, my eyes black pools capped by quick staccato lines for eyebrows. The rest of me is made of big, arching gestures: meaty arms, a strong neck, bumps of drapery. Believe me, I'm no Michelangelo.

I was drawn on the canvas for *The Miracle of the Loaves and Fishes*, part of a group of figures standing around while Jesus makes food for thousands from just a few loaves of bread and a couple of sardines.

Tintoretto left me out of the finished painting. A last-minute change in composition. But I'm still there, underneath that miracle, below that painted surface.

No one recognizes me. Not even the curators from the European Paintings Department or the conservators who have examined me in infrared scans.

I am part of the Met's collection, yet totally invisible.

I came down to the cafeteria to help the staff, to comfort them. A year ago, two curators stood near my painting mourning the destruction of an Italian sculpture of Adam. They wept as they recalled the crash. The brutal, pulverizing crash. I imagined the staff's grief. A death in the collection needed kindness and empathy and a figure on which to lean, even a hastily sketched one. Could broken lines repair broken hearts over broken marble? I was going to try.

Early the next morning, I pushed past the surface of Tintoretto's painting into the museum. It was like passing through a puddle, slipping into the dark water, and coming out the other side. On that first day, I felt so *piccolo*, so exposed. I headed to the Staff Cafeteria where I knew I'd find them.

Pani e pesci, I thought to comfort myself as I tripped on my robe while crossing the empty museum, *it's just loaves and fishes*. I ditched the robe in the cafeteria locker room and, after a little rummaging, *presto*, a uniform.

"*Va bene*," I said as I looked in the mirror, hoping that my 450-year affiliation with those loaves and fishes would translate into some kind of food service experience.

My nametag now says "J.P." I wear it on the black shirt that's part of my uniform. I got J.P. from the wall of donor names on the side of the stairs off the Great Hall.

The "Staff Caf," as they call it, is where they all gather. The staff emerges from their isolated rooms, tucked in corners throughout the museum, to eat and chatter here each day.

It's no *palazzo*, this place. A bunch of low-ceilinged rooms below the Egyptian Galleries filled with bland chairs and tables, including one room with a fountain, where people used to smoke. It has an area that serves hot food and another that serves cold. A salad bar, coffee station, and special theme days, like *Mexico!* or *Strawberries!* Everyone complains about the stomachaches.

But when filled, the dull atmosphere is brightened by a kind of carbonated conversation: warm and gossipy. *Famiglia.* The talk stretches between tables and across departments to keep inaccurate stories alive. These tales swell into a shared mythology. I've overheard them all: covert romances, dubious decisions, demanding donors, the night-shift antics of a guard called Radish.

My affection for the staff blossomed quickly. I love them all. The weird ones. The rude ones. The funny, cheap, and grumbly ones. The stylish ones, the chatty ones, the generous, short, and tired ones.

I once saw one of the skinny girls fall in her super-high heels right near the mashed potatoes. She slid like a cartoon character, until a guard caught her just before she hit the ground. Her skirt flew up and inverted around her waist, like one of those cones you see on the head of a dog. I love her, too.

The other cashiers don't see what I see.

They don't feel the way I do about the staff.

And the staff knows it, like a crush across any cafeteria. When you're walking with your tray, and someone's watching you, even if you're not interested, you know they're there. When they tease you, you feel that crush like a swinging pillow to the head.

They all wonder about me. I catch them looking. They know I see them as they really are.

I listen to the curator of Byzantine art explain a complex theory she has about why someone was hired in the Director's Office. She's trained in messy histories told through intricate objects. For her, everything bends to a complicated plot, with secret chambers hiding pilgrimage treasure.

I like to think of the archaeologists in pith helmets with Indiana Jones whips, gathering treasure as a huge boulder rolls behind them, propelled by some ancient curse. But I hear them talking about volume thirty-two of their cuneiform text translations and know it's all more serious than that.

The guys who change the lightbulbs—the "lampers"—always have light still blazing in their pockets and smeared across their uniforms. The brightness gets trapped under their fingernails, too.

The Department of Photographs sits together every day like a group portrait commemorating some daily, fairy-tale Thanksgiving.

There's a tiny old man who organizes the Met shopping bags in a basement hallway. He has long, thin threads of hair bound with hundreds of rubber bands forming an inch-wide stick down his back. No one's ever seen him outside the building. I'm always nice to him. He leaves rubber bands everywhere he goes, like a trail of breadcrumbs leading back to his colossal paper bag mountain. It is said that he lives there in great splendor.

Sometimes the people who manage the museum's money come in quickly, but they always leave to eat at their desks. They are different. They know they scare the others.

I'm not part of the staff's conversations. I only have a moment with them, so we have a different relationship. And as with any Italian love affair, there must be seduction.

At first, I am distant with each one, transparent with my judgment, curt with my responses. Chilly.

"A lot today," I say aloud to myself as I tally their tray-load of food, like I've been tracking them for a while. A few noises, like, "hmmm..." or a simple, be-mused *"allora"* always rattle them a little. Total silence sends them spinning.

Despite this judgment, I watch them specifically pick my line—one of four to choose from—and slide their plastic trays along the grooved metal counter toward me. They stare at me, the shy side-glance of the beloved, for as long as they can until they think they'll get caught. It's always two seconds too long.

Then, one day—sometimes it takes months—I think, *basta*. It's time. The hard-to-get routine must yield to unbridled charm. It begins simply, but with a happy urgency.

"Have a good day, baby," I say sweetly, and a little loud. They are startled and then pretend that's normal.

"You, too," they shoot back hesitantly. And then they go tell their friends.

I keep it coming.

"I like your pants."

"You look good today, honey."

"You have a nice weekend."

"Baby, where you get that shirt?"

The abruptness and lack of escape makes for a kind of intimacy.

And I wait for them to love me back.

They don't see me yet, but I dream that someday they'll know me for the half-finished drawing that I really am. Because, hey, aren't we all a little *non-finito*?

For now, I'll keep showing up every day and slipping back under the blanket of my painting each night—secretly knowing that the staff is just like me. They appear in the Staff Caf like I appear on those infrared scans—obvious, undeniable. And then they disappear, melting back beneath the painting of the museum, quietly anonymous in their making and their doing.

Until the next day, when we all reappear in that basement again. They load their trays, swap their stories, and stare at me—one more time—for just a little longer than they should.

FOUND

It was just past noon when Virginia Gerard emerged from the empty English period rooms with plans to head out to the steps for a cigarette. She saw the abandoned briefcase alongside the bench. She had been trained for this situation, but now questioned the protocol.

What if someone just left their briefcase there? What if they only went to the bathroom? *What's the big deal*, she thought to herself.

But she knew there would be trouble if she didn't follow procedure, and she couldn't afford to lose this job or its health insurance. Unlike many guards, this was not Virginia's "day job." This was her job. She was not a conceptual artist or fiction writer or ukulele player. She was a single mother with gnawed fingernails chiseled by the lasting disquiet of struggle.

Virginia liked the authority of being a guard. In those galleries, she did not feel small and pitied and watched. In the museum, she did the watching. She did the protecting. She had the answers.

But she was no hero. She just wanted a cigarette.

Virginia waited a moment to see if someone would come and collect the briefcase. Leaning against the wall, annoyed by the intrusion into her break, she wondered if she could pretend she hadn't even seen it.

When no one appeared—and after considering the security cameras that would have tracked her staring at the case—she walked toward the Medieval Hall and picked up the in-house phone to dial 4000.

"Command Center," the supervisor said immediately.

"Um, uh, hi. I'm on break, but there's a large briefcase left in the gallery between the Medieval Hall and the Lehman Wing. I think we're supposed to tell you when that happens?"

She emphasized the break, naively hoping he might tell her to go ahead and leave it to him.

"Are you a security officer?" the supervisor asked curtly.

"Oh, yeah. Sorry. I should have said that," Virginia replied.

"Anyone around there? See anyone who could claim it?" the supervisor continued.

"No, I don't see anyone. I've been watching it for about five minutes to see if someone would come get it."

"And where exactly is it?" he pressed further.

"It's next to a bench in the gallery west of the Medieval Hall, between the French and English period rooms," Virginia explained.

"OK, let me get it up on the screen." He scrolled through the camera views until the gallery was on the central monitor. "Yep, I've got situational awareness on it now."

Virginia rolled her eyes at the tough-guy CIA lingo the Met security chiefs loved to use.

The supervisor zoomed in on the worn briefcase, then took a deep breath before continuing.

"OK, what's your name?" he asked.

"Virginia Gerard."

"OK, Virginia. You're going to do exactly what I tell you."

"OK."

"First, go back to the briefcase and rope off that gallery from the Medieval Hall, the French period rooms, and the English period rooms. That will isolate the area. Then, go into the Lehman Wing and get the other guards—I think Dave is back there today.

"You're going to sweep those galleries and get everyone out of there via the ground floor service exit. I can't see anyone in there on my screens, but I may be missing people. You should be able to clear the galleries and go out through the basement at 84th Street. Move any visitors to the street and then come to the front steps to be redeployed. Got it?"

"Yes, sir. Are we, uh, evacuating?" Virginia asked with a tone that suggested that this was somehow her fault. She just wanted a cigarette.

There was a pause before he answered, but she knew already.

"You're damn right we're evacuating," he said just before hanging up.

Virginia did as she was told, and soon the usual *klop-klop* of visitors walking on the museum's stone floors was replaced by the buzz and commotion of hundreds of footsteps moving toward the Fifth Avenue entrance. The practice of polite whispering had also been abandoned, and a wave of echoed complaints tumbled through the galleries.

Even the art speculated about this jolt to the Met's usual rhythm. The tapestries that surrounded the briefcase regarded it with disdain—a rat in a connoisseur's kitchen. Some objects remembered when they themselves were evacuated during World War II, ninety truckloads filled with works of art packed up like children, sent to live on an estate outside Philadelphia, where they stayed for two years. Safe in their crates, but blinded from one another, they longed for home and the release of being unpacked and displayed, air and visitors floating around them again.

Now, the displaced swarm streamed past the art and out of the museum, confused and irritated, sloppily spilling from all three sets of doors at the top of the Fifth Avenue steps, like commuters from a broken-down bus.

The staff connected lazily within the throng, got food for lunch, and gossiped, sharing conflicting explanations for what was happening. The locals shrugged with a detached cool, signaling that they could come back anytime. The tourists consulted their guidebooks, happy to replace the Met with another attraction nearby. Walter considered the mess that this slow stampede would leave behind on his steps.

The suburban ladies in their pantsuits and carefully tied scarves held the most ire. They planned their museum visits like military operations, with prescribed train times, lunch reservations, and advanced reading. They tensely gripped their handbag straps at their shoulders and clucked about not renewing their Met memberships.

In the final years of the twentieth century, fear was not yet a reflex. The whole thing was just a hassle, an interruption of plans. Within two years, the Met's vulnerability would shift to a constant concern. Crowds scrutinized. Entrances watched. Bags checked. No one would hesitate about an abandoned briefcase again.

Bruno Parker watched the evacuation from the top of the steps with a seasoned calm. His approach was pragmatic: Each person who passed through the doors was another individual out of danger. His radio clicked alive with a report muzzled by static: "We've secured the perimeter."

He looked to his right, where his steely boss, Dick Trachner, stood next to him, and nodded with affirmation that the museum's security protocol was proceeding as planned.

Melvin's briefcase would be mangled by the bomb-sniffing dogs who were summoned by the police. It would be removed from the museum, put in an armored truck, and brought to the NYPD Bomb Squad on Charles Street.

Inside it, they would find only blank paper.

Farther south, down on Varick Street, an unemployment counselor would shout Melvin's name into a room filled with orange plastic chairs, hear no response, and move to the next person on his list.

Virginia would sit on the steps and finally have her cigarette, not realizing that they had just rehearsed for a day, not long away, when the world would shatter.

THE TALENT

Nick, I love you, but I am hanging up the phone. I promise, I'll figure this out." Click.

Nick slumps in his chair as he hears this and knows she's right. She will protect him. But his instinct is always to fret, always to worry about what is not said, what he doesn't know, what is coming, lurking, looming.

In the third grade, his teacher asked her students to bring in an old magazine for an art project, and he could barely sleep that night. He wondered if he should take his grandfather's *Field & Stream* (more socially acceptable) or his mother's *House & Garden* (better images). What would everyone else bring? What were they going to be asked to *do* with it? What was *the plan*?

He settled on an issue of *TIME*. They were instructed to use the magazines to make a collage that visualized a colloquial expression. He pasted the figure of a tiny woman under a large image of Jackie Kennedy's mouth and connected the two with a hooked handle to illustrate "Let a smile be your umbrella." It was a phrase his mother would repeat dismissively when he sulked about being excluded at recess. She had long ago labeled him an Eeyore for his sullen anxiety. He still thinks she gave bullshit advice.

Nick pushes back from his chair and wonders if it's time for lunch. He stares at the face of his watch as if it's in another language, one that he used to know, but now struggles with. It is only 10:30. He decides to go to the Staff Cafeteria for a coffee, more for the comfort than the caffeine.

I can't shake you today. You're like a bad penny," Julia says with a smile from behind him at the coffee station. She is tall and capable, in a no-nonsense "I-know-more-than-you-need-to-know" way. "Sorry I hung up on you, but you have to trust me. I'll get you the gallery space."

"I know, I know, but someone told me that Marta already got the B Galleries for her Middle Kingdom show, and I really can't have my pictures hanging on eleven-foot-high walls in Service Building B. The work needs to breathe, and I promised all the lenders that *we* were in the B Galleries."

"Heard it all this morning, Nick," Julia sings, her voice trailing off as she walks away with her tea. "Good morning, J.P.," she adds, greeting the cashier. Nick realizes Julia has moved on and quickens his pace to get behind her. "I'll pay for this gentleman's coffee, too. He needs a break."

"OK, baby. You looking good today." J.P. winks at Julia, ignoring Nick.

"No, no, I got it." Nick reaches for his wallet with a jolt, as if he's just woken up to what's happening. He is unfailingly nervous about money.

"It'll be fine, Nick," Julia snaps, "Like I said on the phone, let me take care of it."

"The coffee or the galleries?"

"Both! Argh. Just give me a day." The frustration in her voice is clear, but tinged with affection. They have been here before.

"OK, OK. Call me when you know anything."

She turns her head and rolls her eyes with a smile, a gesture that reassures him of her devotion.

"Or if I can help!" he yells after her.

She is on her way now, advancing with quick, deliberate strides, calling over her shoulder, "You can't."

He looks up and sees Dave, a guard he's known for fifteen years and who has witnessed this exchange.

"Don't mess with her, man," Dave offers, "She'll do what she says. Always does." He has seen a lot standing in those galleries, heard a lot in this cafeteria.

"I know, I know. But my pictures cannot hang in rooms with ten-foot ceilings," Nick says, a little excited to have a new audience for his complaint. That may actually be why he came down to the basement cafeteria. Everyone in his department has heard his grumbling already, and agrees with him. He needs fresh ears.

"She won't let that happen," Dave replies and turns away, "My break's over. See you in the Petrie Court."

Nick looks at his coffee and realizes he forgot to add milk. He heads to the milk station and scans the room for anyone else he might buttonhole over his issue, but the breakfast rush has passed, and it's too early for the lunch crowd. The room is empty except for a huddle of riggers getting ready to move a monumental Egyptian statue. At another table, some technology guys in matching fleece and khakis talk about cabling. Not his people.

He could go upstairs and call his husband. He won't want to hear it, but he's legally obligated to listen. *No, he won't have the right passion for the problem*, Nick thinks. Only another curator will understand.

He dials the head of the Medieval Department, but gets voicemail. He tries Katrina in Asian Art, but is told she is in London to preview the auctions. On his third try, he gets Tim, the head of Paintings Conservation, who is empathetic and patient, but hardly delivers the requisite outrage.

"I'm sure Julia will figure it out. I know it's hard, but just let her do her thing."

"I know, I know, but how does this even happen? I'm told one thing at one time, and another thing later, and I just don't know how we are supposed to function like this. I feel like we never know what's going on. My pictures cannot hang on nine-foot walls."

Tim sits on the other end of the phone and scans eBay for Staffordshire figurines to add to his personal collection. Nick's rant unfurls into a looping commentary that is both absurd and self-sustaining. He inventories every conspiracy theory he has hatched about why he is being assigned the low-ceilinged Service Building B instead of the grand B Galleries for his show.

Tim clicks "Add to Cart" on a flawless porcelain cow creamer, and listens. He has served this purpose before, the role of the empathetic ear. He is known as a benevolent colleague for his ability to appear concerned by saying very little.

"Let me know if there is anything I can do," Tim finally interrupts after ten minutes. "I'm happy to chime in if it would be helpful." It's the longest Tim has spoken during the call, but it's all Nick will remember.

After they finish, Nick puts his head in his hands and registers again that he is losing his hair. He has just turned fifty, and the displacement of volume from his head to his midsection is a growing trend, one only accelerated by his current stress. He left Minnesota at nineteen with a nerdy charm—wavy dark hair and the nose of a Roman senator—at odds with the Nordic looks of the corn-fed boys at his high school. But in the east coast world of pasty academics and bookish intellectuals, he was a bright and handsome Midwesterner: F. Scott Fitzgerald without the complicated wife. That new status alone propelled him to pursue his PhD. Now, the gradual dimming of that early star is devastating. His gaze lands on his shirt buttons, small fortifications straining to contain his stomach's unscheduled expansion.

He knows he should call Mrs. Havering to continue his charm offensive. She could pay for both the exhibition and the catalog. And if she were the show's sponsor, there is no way they would move him out of the B Galleries. The price is a near-daily phone call to listen to her whinge about the world's slights against her.

Nick is willing to indulge her; he knows that much of his success has been tied to his consistent ability to entice the right patrons and collectors. But he needs an angle for Havering. He looks at the exhibition checklist on his desk, the inventory of every work of art he wants for the show, and decides to give her an update on the loans. He finds her number on a sticky note attached to his phone, a constant reminder to call and cajole.

After several rings, a voice says, "Haver-bing-ah reseedi-dence." The accent is thick, but its origins unclear.

"Hello. Is Mrs. Havering at home? This is Nick Morton from the Metropolitan Museum."

No response follows. Instead, the phone clatters on the kitchen counter and then drags across the granite until it falls to the floor. Nick can envision the phone itself, a yellowing, rotary dial, Park Avenue relic installed in the early 1980s.

"Hello? Who is this?" Mrs. Havering sounds skeptical that anyone is really on the phone.

He hears the maid's quick, heavy breathing through the kitchen phone before she bangs it back into its cradle.

"Mrs. Havering. It's Nick...Nick Morton, from the Met."

"Oh, hello. What do you want?"

Nick is not surprised by the brusque tone; it is always the same, and makes the tempo to every conversation with Havering uneasy.

"I thought you would be excited to hear that we got the loans from Berlin. They are giving us every painting we asked for."

"Well, I'm not sure why I would want to know that, but OK," she stammers with cynical force, then tries to be positive. She likes Nick. "That's good news. It is. You know I was supposed to go to Berlin last year, but I didn't."

This, too, is typical of Havering. She has a way of interjecting information without participating in the standard protocol of fleshing out any kind of story around it. There is no back and forth, just forth. Nick should recognize his own twin in this style, but doesn't.

"Uh, sorry to hear that—" he searches, wondering if this is the right approach.

"Well, I didn't *want* to go. If I *did*, I would have gone."

"Of course," he stabilizes, but knows he will capsize again. He will not bring up the gallery situation for fear of completely sinking.

"If that's all you want to tell me, I have to go. I have a board meeting at Lincoln Center so they can show me how *ungrateful* they are for my generosity. *Again*." Click.

It is the second time someone has hung up on Nick today. He sits holding the phone, listening to the lights buzz above him as he looks around his office. The desk and table overflow with books and papers in a system he alone claims to understand. He has nested here over the last two decades.

Havering makes him think of his own mother, who has spiraled into an equally tyrannical grouch at age eighty-one. When she last visited, she removed the flowers from her room, telling him, "I don't need these," as she dropped the vase on the kitchen counter with a dull thump. "Let a smile be your umbrella!" he should have said.

Nick suddenly realizes he is ten minutes late for the Dry Run and races down the hallway, taking the stairs to the second floor and skirting past visitors to cross the Nineteenth-Century Paintings Galleries toward the Boardroom elevator. By the time he reaches the Rodin galleries, he realizes he is the source of the panting sound he hears. He slows down to an uneven, hustling gait, so that he is not visibly sweating when he arrives.

The meeting is a dress rehearsal for the Trustee Acquisitions Meeting, where objects are presented to be purchased for the collection. This Dry Run phase is a peer-review process, and much more intimidating than the actual Trustees. Curators can be ruthless or supportive, and ultimately make recommendations to the Director, who decides which objects will move forward.

Nick makes a loud entrance, the kind that is inevitable when hoping not to be noticed, activating every squeak and thud available in the double doors of the cavernous boardroom. As he moves inside he nearly knocks over a four-thousand-year-old Cycladic terracotta jug, one of the objects installed for review around the perimeter of the room.

He then abandons any attempt at stealth.

"Sorry I'm late," he says to the entire room. As he circles the enormous table to find an empty seat, he unspools his thoughts. "What a day. I was just on the phone with Mona Havering, and boy is she hard work. And now my exhibition galleries are being taken away. Julia says she's going to figure it out, but I don't know what's going on. I can't show my pictures in galleries with eight-foot ceilings. And I've got to go to London next week. I'm sorry I'm wearing my old glasses, but I couldn't find the new ones this morning after the dog ran into the elevator of our building, and I had to chase after him."

He piles these random laments like a small house of cards, steadily placing one complaint on top of the other, as if curious where the tipping point might actually be. The others watch this theater patiently, struck by the arrogance of Nick's running commentary, but well accustomed to their colleague's half-empty worldview.

A deep baritone intercedes to halt the soliloquy, "Nick. If you are quite finished, we might proceed with the meeting," Michel Larousse intones, short-fused by the interruption. "Peter, go ahead."

"Right. Sorry," Nick apologizes sheepishly.

He only now notices that his friend Peter Geldman is already standing in front of the assembled curators.

He is about to propose a Jim Campbell video of a walking man. On an LED screen the size of a television, the diffused silhouette of a figure is seen from the side casting a long shadow, walking with infinite steps as if on some invisible treadmill.

Peter looks at the video and waits so that his audience must also linger on its rhythm. He uncharacteristically wears a gray suit, a costume that has hung for sixteen years on the back of his office door and which makes no sense on his sloping frame. The top button of his shirt is undone, the small split forming an arrow to the mangled knot that defines his tie, pulled hard to the left as if trying to escape the awkward situation of the whole outfit.

Peter is both nervous and untouchable, the curse and blessing of those who choose to introduce anything avant-garde to the Met. The crowd will inevitably be resistant and wary of wandering into such unknown turf.

As he speaks, Peter clutches the fabric of his lapels, making his hands into tight fists. He then pushes inward and upward as if squeezing the ideas out of his chest, so that they spill from his mouth. What is then said is in total opposition to this contorted visual presentation. He speaks with crisp clarity—and disarming strength.

"This is Jim Campbell's *Motion and Rest #2* from 2002. In this series, Campbell is examining the ways that digital technology transforms the nature of perception and subjective experience. His art combines an MIT education in mathematics and electrical engineering with a keen historical awareness of the relationship these two fields have with earlier visual media, particularly photography and film.

"For the *Motion and Rest* series, the artist took as inspiration the stop-motion photographs of Eadweard Muybridge from the 1880s. These were works that simultaneously furthered scientific understanding of the human body and, by extension, prepared it for the rote techniques of assembly-line production developed at the same moment by industrial engineer Frederick Taylor.

"Campbell's updated versions are wall-mounted panels composed of hundreds of tiny white LED lights through which is fed looped footage of figures walking in profile, and whose outlines are composed of the negative space left by the undulating ripples of white light that define their contours.

"This application of a black-and-white dot matrix relates them to yet another development of the 1880s: the halftone method of photographic reproduction in which many of Muybridge's motion studies first appeared."

Peter pauses, letting them absorb these ideas before his ending.

"But look closely. Unlike Muybridge's well-built, agile human specimens, Campbell's subjects hobble and lurch before stopping to rest and catch their breath—the result of various disabilities such as limps or severe arthritis. They perform an implicit, ironic rebuke to any blind faith in technology's mythic link to progress and human fulfillment.

"There is a mesmerizing social commentary built within the work's visual poetry."

Peter finishes by letting go of his lapels, part release, part challenge. His colleagues are struck by his brevity and his confidence. What looked to them like a rudimentary video game has now emerged as something quite different. They see connections to the movement suggested in the earliest Greek kouros, the linear evocations of action in Egyptian hieroglyphs, the repetition of patterns in the paintings of Cy Twombly, the revealed narratives of Chinese scroll painting, the social caricature of Hogarth, and the agrarian nostalgia of Winslow Homer's post–Civil War paintings. Any hesitation they had about the validity of this video as art is now set aside, replaced with an acquiescence that the museum should acquire it.

Nick watches this unfold, and wonders if the ungainliness of Peter's performance is part of a clever strategy. Peter may just be shrewd enough to understand the effective distraction of his own graceless appearance when coupled with the charisma of his extraordinary mind.

Michel is unenthusiastic, but cannot argue with the pithy arc of Peter's presentation; he asks if anyone has questions and is met with silence. No one will dare wrestle with Peter's expertise in the risky territory of contemporary video. Some curators are great scholars, others great exhibition makers, still others, superb collectors. It is rare to have a curator like Peter, who excels at all three.

As the meeting continues with the Cycladic vase, Nick looks across the table at a Greek and Roman scholar with a near photographic memory who has spent her forty-two-year career pursuing the endless puzzle of reconstructing ancient Greek vases. Somehow that path seems simpler than the more showy, ambitious one that Nick has chosen with big exhibitions, high-powered donors, and a growing profile both within and outside the museum.

Perhaps he did it all wrong? He stews on that larger idea, magnifying it into an existential crisis, until he removes his glasses to scratch his nose and shifts seamlessly back to thoughts of the dog in the elevator. This is Nick's peculiar gift: the ability to escape the downward spiral of his own instincts by worrying about anything and everything simultaneously.

The video of the walking man has been moved to the side, but is still playing. Nick stares at it, hypnotized. *He* is the walking man—going nowhere despite his constant efforts.

He looks back at the Greek vase specialist and considers the puzzle that has been wrought around his show's galleries going to Marta instead of him.

He decides he must craft some plan of attack. Marta is not in the meeting so this could be the ideal time to rally others around this injustice. Or Michel. If only Nick could catch him afterward, though Michel is known for his swift exits through the catering door.

When the meeting finally ends, Nick's strategy of rallying his colleagues is thwarted by gossip about a donor photoshoot in Paintings Conservation, a story that consumes the group as Tim recounts it with typical animation.

"I know the drill, lady. Shoulders back! Tits out!" Tim mocks, exaggerating the donor's pose for the photographer with a twist of his own body. His colleagues roar with laughter.

Impatiently grasping for some empathy, Nick bets on the Staff Cafeteria again now that it's lunchtime. As he crosses the Ancient Near East Galleries he sees Alexander Ferris, his exhibition's press officer. Alexander's youth and startling good looks do little to pacify Nick's sense of his own diminishing attractiveness, but Ferris's impenetrable swagger could come in handy. Maybe a press release has been sent out announcing that his show will be in the B Galleries?

"Alexander!" Nick shouts toward the Gates of Nineveh.

Alexander turns, distracting one of the groups of religious tourists who tend to be the sole occupants of the Ancient Near East Galleries. The visitors are beguiled by his beauty, following his every move as if an idealized sculpture has come to life before them. They are strikingly unfazed by the fact that a man is yelling in the otherwise silent space.

"Nick," Alexander hums as the frenetic curator catches up to him. Proximity to Alexander's height and ease immediately and irrationally calm Nick. "What's up?" Alexander asks.

"Has my press release gone out?" Nick asks breathlessly, as if there is a typo in an artist's name.

"No, you have the draft. We're waiting on your comments."

"Oh, right. Of course." Nick replies, now deflated. "I'll…I'll get it to you. It's just that I heard that my exhibition is being moved to Service Building B, and if the journalists were already expecting the show to be in the B Galleries, then we really can't move it."

Alexander tilts his head as if listening to a small child tell him about a monster under the bed.

"Well, I'm not sure that would be the case anyway. Let's hope the journalists don't ever have that kind of power, but Julia will handle it," Alexander lulls. "These things always sort themselves out."

"Right. I know, but I can't show my pictures in a gallery with seven-foot ceilings."

Once again, Nick's refrain does not produce the desired fury.

"It'll be fine," Alexander assures. "I have to dash to meet someone in the Great Hall for lunch. Let me know what happens."

"Yeah, OK." Nick says, defeated.

"Eye of the tiger, my friend," Alexander encourages with his signature line—which works not for its poetry, but for the astonishing magnetism of the person delivering it.

As Nick enters the Staff Cafeteria he sees Marta's tiny frame out of the corner of his eye. She fills the birdlike proportions of a young girl, but maintains the demeanor of a deposed dictator: At any time, she might be quietly wrangling a small army for a retaliatory coup d'état. He must avoid her in case she asks about the B Galleries. Or worse, claims them as hers without apology, sealing his low-ceilinged fate.

Nick stands frozen in the entry and thinks he might want to run. The cafeteria is cleaved into two halves, one for hot food and one for cold. Marta stands with her tray on the hot side waiting patiently for her ladle full of the *Mexico!* special. She is not prepared for the unenthusiastic "Olé" that accompanies the sound of wet beans hitting the dry paper plate.

"Excuse me?" she questions in her galloping German accent. "*Vas?*" But the unhappy ladler has moved on.

Nick grabs a plastic tray and holds it over his face as he slips into the cold food side. He approaches the salad bar and panics as he sees Marta now coming toward him. Desperate, Nick burrows his face toward a vat of carrot salad, as if he's lost something in the stringy orange glop. It reeks of dill and vinegar.

"You must really like carrots," Peter Geldman jokes as he slaps Nick on the back, bouncing his head forward, and lodging a small sticky piece of dill between his nostrils.

"Good presentation," Nick muffles into the carrots, as Peter moves on.

Nick feels Marta at his back reviewing the salad bar.

"Look at all zee meats and cheeses," Marta comments aloud as she walks past him. She delivers her observation with surprise, as if the cold cuts are dipped in gold. He hears victory in her voice. The lenses of her enormous glasses seem drawn toward the sandwich station; they miss—or more likely ignore—Nick.

When he thinks it's clear, Nick clutches his still-empty tray and moves to the soda fountain to avoid Marta's sightline as she heads to the cashier. He focuses intently on filling his cup with ice, then adds some Diet Coke while he stares at the machine's worn, sputtering spigot.

When Marta has paid, Nick scuttles to the hot side, a restless beetle dodging the crush of a boot. He grabs a pre-made tuna sandwich and drops it into a paper bag at the register, so he can avoid the seating area and eat in the safety of his department.

He shifts his eyes sideways to see where Marta is sitting, but she has moved on, perhaps to another room. She is so slight she could be perched on a windowsill nibbling her food like a squirrel.

After making a U-turn to leave through the cafeteria entrance, Nick traverses the museum underground, tense with the possibility that Marta will appear in his path. He passes the old dumbwaiter and is sure she could fit in there, ready to pounce.

At last, Nick sits at the table in his office, inhaling the consoling smell of old books. He is not even hungry. Maybe he could call Carl, the compassionate head librarian, and tell him about the low ceilings? But the desk seems far away after Nick's outlay of frantic energy this morning. He is relieved to be back in his office, but sure his fate is sealed.

He remembers how he used to escape a bully named William at school by eating lunch in the principal's office. William once asked Nick to join his table in the cafeteria, then pulled the chair away as Nick sat down. He laid on the floor like a starfish, blinking away tears under a tent of howling faces. Nick's stomach still flips at the thought of the humiliation.

That vulnerability has never left him, the pressing fear that things will be taken away from him: chairs, lunchrooms, galleries, control. Nick's mother used to take away his World Book Encyclopedias to force him to play with the other boys on his block. "Get some fresh air, some rough and tumble," she would plead. He would go outside to placate her, baffled by her "rough and tumble" aspirations for him, then promptly repel the other children with tedious, exhaustive descriptions of the world, as remembered from his confiscated books: entries on the Russian Revolution, or Charles Lindbergh, or Nick's favorite section, the Mylar pages showing layers of dissected frogs and human innards. It was perhaps the first time that he realized that some things simply needed to be seen. And that success sometimes rests on *how* they're seen: Mylar pages, ceiling heights, it *all* matters.

At 1:00 PM, the phone rings, and he can see it's Julia.

"Hey. What's the news?" he quivers.

"Done," she says without a hello.

"Wait. How? What is Marta going to do?"

"Nick, it's done. Everyone's happy. Stop worrying. The B Galleries are yours."

Her tone is that of a sister delivering the family's decision about who will host Thanksgiving. Nick knows that Julia understands that his needy arrogance and fretting are anchored in the same dedication to the Met that she herself feels. They have grown up together in this museum. It is a kind of trust that spreads across all the old-timers, the unbreakable bond of an unchanging cast.

"Uh, thank God. Thank you." Nick sighs with relief.

"Anytime," she replies. "You're the talent. And the Director's Office aims to please."

"Well, you've got a satisfied customer."

"Only 101 more to go," she adds with a laugh, referring to the full staff of 102 curators.

Only three hours have passed since their first call this morning, but Nick has packed a year's worth of agonizing into that time. He shoves his anxiety into every second of every minute, like jamming extra socks into an overstuffed suitcase.

"Drinks at the Stanhope on Friday?" he asks, now cheered.

"Done."

Six months later, the B Galleries are empty at 8:00 PM except for the 184 pictures that lean against the walls of the nine rooms in an initial configuration for the exhibition. Couriers from across the globe have brought the works of art to this space, inspected them, and left them in the museum's care. The technicians will start hanging the paintings in the morning. Folding screens block the entrance to the galleries where tomorrow a guard will sit all day, allowing only authorized staff to enter after signing in. A credit line on the title wall reads, "Made possible, in part, by Mrs. Leonard Havering."

Nick stands in the space he was so fearful of losing. He feels a calm that only arrives in moments like these, when he and the art have nothing between them. He rests his gaze on each painting like an old friend, comforted by the same excitement and familiarity that marks any passionate reunion. He has seen each work before in its home, but now assumes the role of host to this gathering.

"Oh, hello lovely," he says tenderly as he kneels to look at a portrait of a young girl. Her eyes sink with a knowingness that seems to portend some tragic fate. Her hands clutch each other to reveal a strain beyond her years. She is at once fresh and ancient, the very essence of Nick himself in the guise of an eighteenth-century child.

This is the dream. To stand before the weight and heft of the real things, not reproductions or high-definition scans, but the objects themselves, touched by the artist's hand, *made* by human effort, skill, and ambition. The centuries traversed between that creation and Nick's lifetime are made irrelevant by an immediacy that is overpowering here, on this night, in this gloaming, charged with Nick's own, glimmering spark.

His hands slip into his pockets as he walks quietly through each room, a father beholding his sleeping children. What is laid out on the floor is what was specified in the original, chronological exhibition design, but it is different than what is now mapped in Nick's head.

He has changed his approach from that early plan, and he will fix it. His new version will more closely mirror the conversation that has unfolded in his mind over years of research and contemplation, two decades of thinking about what this show could be—visually, sensually, intellectually. He will ignore chronology and use subject and style to structure the show instead.

It is part class reunion, part dinner party: the juxtaposition of pictures that have known the same maker, but never the same room. Only a curator can imagine this meeting and then actually construct it. The unraveling of a life's work to build a story for the world to see.

Nick pulls his hands from his pockets and folds them over his chest. It is a gesture of silence, a pause before a swelling momentum. In his head there is not music, but a steady beat, one that pulses along with the intensity of his anticipation.

He begins. In his mind, the first picture floats through the dark to the south wall, the opening salvo to the exhibition. It is followed by the next painting swiftly landing where Nick has always envisioned it, alongside the first self-portrait drawing, revealing how the quality of line never really changed from that earliest work.

Nick sorts it out all in his head, imagining each object dangling in the air and then gliding into just the right slot. He blinks and shifts his eyes back and forth, dreaming of the works flashing from one spot to another—one room to another—with the rolling precision of a dancer dipping inevitably into the next step of an improvised movement.

There is an elegance that circles this quiet shuffling. The tangled, worried Nick has disappeared. In his place is a graceful illusionist, able to see what others will only realize once he is finished. Every grievance, every complaint, fades in the face of the marvel he can conjure in these rooms.

He's simply worth the trouble.

Nick decides the placement of the last picture around 1:00 AM. He leans against a doorway and thinks about his Greek vase colleague: this instant must be what it feels like to slip an ancient shard into its long-lost vacancy.

He is drained and exhilarated by his new plan, buzzing with a spiraling high. He secretly knows the art will rescue him every time, even if tonight he didn't need its magic. Before he leaves, he looks around with satisfaction, registering the height of the ceiling with a lingering sense of triumph.

A week later, with every picture now hanging, Nick clutches the phone with rage and dials Julia's number.

"Mr. Morton!" Julia welcomes, "The installation is beautiful. You must be thrilled."

"Julia," he begins tightly, despite knowing that this issue is not really her responsibility. "I am look-ing at the menu for my opening reception, and there are only almonds. I was promised cashews." His voice manages to pick up speed while simultaneously extending the underlying whine. "I don't know how this happened. Last March, I had a meeting with Special Events and they asked"—his exasperation becomes mocking—"'Nick, what would you like to serve at your opening?' and I said, 'Just make sure there are cashews.' Now I see that they have *completely* ignored that request. I mean, what is going *on* here? Are there even going to be drinks? I feel like I have no idea what is happening around my own show!"

Eeyore is back. And they have taken away his cashews.

"What's Mona Havering going to do?" he continues, "Munch on a bunch of almonds like she's on a business-class flight? I was at the Asian Art Friends event two weeks ago and they had cashews—*a lot of them*. I remember the last time I ordered a cheese plate from Special Events, and we got a giant hunk of cheddar with a big hole cut in the middle stuffed with crackers. It looked like...like *casserole night* at the Elks Lodge!...Julia?...Julia?"

Julia's voice lowers into her most "I-know-more-than-you-know" tone.

"You know what, Nick...," she replies slowly and with perfect sincerity, hinting that she has just figured out the root of this dreadful cashew crime. A sense of revelation soaks her words.

"Maybe *Marta* got your cashews?" she suggests with a tinge of horror.

Before he can answer, he hears the distant ring of Julia's laughter. She sounds even farther away when she teases him with the phrase she knows he hates most.

"Let a smile be your umbrella!" echoes from the phone. The fading words are followed by another, more familiar sound: *Click.*

WHAT WE WONDERED ABOUT
ALEXANDER FERRIS

We wondered how he came to us. How his fair-haired ease slipped into a job in the Communications Office. He was a fresh, gleaming apple amid the gloom of ringing phones and broken office chairs.

We wondered about his beauty. He could release it like a slingshot, showering us with its delicate, shimmering force: a Staff Caf Achilles without the wonky heel, a marble Adam before the fall.

We wondered if he ever touched the ground. Did he glide through the outside world the same way he floated through the museum, effortlessly propelled by some kindly nudging breeze? His pace was rebellious in its calm. No urgency could cling to him, no authority could unsteady his soothing ballast.

We wondered if he was real. If he ever lost keys or bought milk or missed subway trains. In his elegant blue suits and Italian shoes, he quieted the museum's often nervous energy. We fell into his charisma. Sank into its depths until it coated our every surface. We made him gay and straight and secretly married, the leading man of so many great and glamorous affairs.

We wondered if he was even paid, preferring the dream that he was impossibly wealthy. His time with us was a cultural diversion, a professional trifle. He was our Gatsby—minus the unworkable dreams and tragic demise.

We wondered why he stayed.

We wondered about his words. The slow beat of his phrases and crisp, clarion voice. He spoke in the balanced paragraphs taught in elementary school, ending, always, with tidy, punctuated precision.

We wondered where he was from. Once we heard Ohio. Which sounded too ordinary. That he was one of six children. Again, not quite right. We ignored what did not suit our illusions, cherry-picking our details like fresh blooms in a field. Chocolates from a box.

We decided San Francisco. Four children. With standard poodles and a platinum mother (hair and credit). Heiress to some unexpected fortune, pet food or plastic wrap.

We wondered if he liked us. Our cafeteria banter and trite office greeting cards seemed so small against his majesty. But there he was: farewells, weddings, birthdays—all marked with the same cryptic phrase, somehow asserting a relevance no one else could conjure. Four words scribbled in his florid hand, no matter what the occasion: *Eye of the tiger.*

We wondered how long our hero would remain.

After four years, he left. Our golden gladiator, carried down Fifth Avenue one warm October evening. On to Lisbon or Monaco, the Ottoman Empire or fifth-century Athens.

But we did not let him go. We wised up, took over his ghost, and gossiped on. Introduced his foamy celebrity to each new staff member, like some crucial orientation film.

We rolled out his story at every occasion—all those farewells, weddings, birthdays—until it became a museum anthem, sung passionately at each event, bloating his infinite legend, until we were whispering "eye of the tiger" to deathbed retirees.

Curators identified him as Caravaggio's lover, Saint-Gaudens's model for Hiawatha, and Picasso's drinking buddy. Staff, old and new, claimed sightings in the basement, the Japanese Galleries, and the Trustees' Dining Room.

Over time, the pet food empire evolved into a principality itself—Purinoa, a small island nation off the coast of New Zealand—that he now ruled benevolently.

His departure took on intrigue, too, driven by a lustful tryst with either Nick Morton, Helen Winlock, or a guard named Maira. Maybe Zeus. Some say Apollo. Or Aphrodite.

We stood before medieval reliquaries stuffed with an arm bone or a wisdom tooth and sighed, "Yeah, that's his."

We no longer required the thrill of the real Alexander Ferris.

Fantasy Ferris—bigger, brighter, blonder, beautiful-er—had obscured the boy himself. And we wondered no more.

WHERE WE KEEP THE LIGHT

Moody Russell cradled the unwieldy pillow of light in his arms and looked toward the Buddha Gallery's forty-foot-high ceilings as he bent his knees and threw the cloud upward, releasing it into the air. It floated skyward like a stray balloon, then fractured just before reaching the ceiling, a firework display filling each fixture. The gallery lights were on.

Moody was one of the Met's lampers—the guys in charge of changing the lightbulbs.

Sometimes the objects didn't seem ready to face the fresh glare of the coming day: the visitors, the flashbulbs, the constant squeak of tourist chatter. "Aw, come on!," Moody imagined a monumental Buddha moaning. "Five more minutes?" Its tone would be that of a bleating teenager. If the Buddha had a pillow—which, given its size, would need to be the scale of a mattress—it would crush it over its head.

"Sorry, big guy," Moody would say to comfort the Buddha, "but you're the star of this show."

Moody moved to the next gallery, climbing a few steps until he reached the room devoted to the arts of Korea. There, he pulled another armload of light from the supply he carried on his orange cart and threw it more softly toward the lower, eighteen-foot ceilings.

This time, the cloud snagged on a graceful stone hand sculpted into a gesture of meditation. The radiance hung there for a moment until Moody gave the cloud a gentle shove, sending it north and leaving a bright smudge of light across his brown Met uniform. Moody looked down and scowled, knowing that the other lampers would see that he'd missed a shot.

In the Temple of Dendur, Moody took out the broomstick clamped to his cart and swung it at smaller puffs of light. He paused like a home-run hitter watching the luminescence soar upward into the cavernous space. "Aaaaahh!" Moody cried with a hollow yell to emulate the roar of a crowd.

Moody had always been good with light, ever since he grabbed his first moonbeam as a toddler. He cradled it all night in his crib, a secret comfort in the room's frightening eclipse. As a child, he would look out the window of his suburban house and imagine that the outline of the trees formed the inky shadow of a sleeping monster, only kept in its slumber by the shine of nearby streetlights. Later, as a teenager, he would stare at the stars, soothed by their pulsing breath, reassuring flashes in the face of his greatest fear: the dark.

For Moody, darkness was a place, a tunnel where adult voices swelled into anger, then howls and pain. Darkness could hurt.

The door to his room would crack open to reveal the hulking shadow of his father, as if the sleeping monster were now awake. He would drag Moody from his bed so he could shove and bat at the boy's body, scraping and grabbing at his adolescent frame with swinging, extraordinary paws. A brutal roar would echo, rippling to the walls and back again, until the beast was sufficiently fed. Then he would drop the boy to the floor like a worn-out toy, and stagger, panting, from the room.

These nights made Moody skittish and easily broken, often cowering despite his size and unrealized strength. His family mocked the throbbing clench of his terror; they called him "moody."

Light's the whole game!" Moody would now tell anyone at the museum. "Can't see any of this stuff in the dark!"

As he made his stops each morning, Moody let his mind travel—the gray light of Paris, the scorching brightness of ancient Assyria, the summer sky of Wayzata, Minnesota, in the Frank Lloyd Wright room.

His favorite escape was the Gubbio Studiolo, a small private study made for the Duke of Montefeltro's fifteenth-century palace in Gubbio, Italy.

Moody loved the closet-sized room, a complete illusion made with walls constructed of intarsia—tiny shapes of wood pieced together to create the impression of cabinets and shelves, latticed doors and benches. The fantasy continued with renderings of all the attributes of a Renaissance man: armor and military honors, piles of books, and instruments associated with music, science, and architecture.

Every object was depicted with perfect perspective, animated by the further illusion of light and shadow made with different types and tones of wood. Moody understood the constructed shadows like an astronomer could grasp the solar system. They transformed the two dimensions into three, and corresponded to the source of real light in the original room: two windows side-by-side in a niche to the right as you entered.

Moody would often stand in the Studiolo, the Italian sun brilliantly recreated with a series of invisible fixtures set beyond the windows. The false sunlight poured into the room's nestling confines and stretched across the terracotta floor, providing a dizzying comfort in its perpetual afternoon.

Hey Moody Russell!"
Moody heard the thud of Joe Carasi's Staten Island accent across the empty Medieval Hall. He turned to see his fellow lamper tossing mounds of light toward the stained-glass windows from a cherry picker. "What's the difference between a pregnant woman and a light bulb?" Carasi asked.

"What?" Moody Russell yelled back, playing along.

"You can unscrew a light bulb," Carasi replied.

"Hey Joe Carasi," Moody continued, without any reaction to the previous joke, as he pushed his cart slowly across the hall to European Decorative Arts, "How many Roman Catholics does it take to screw in a light bulb?"

"How many?" Carasi said with mocked enthusiasm, as Moody moved past him.

"Two," replied Moody over his shoulder, "One to screw it in and another to repent."

Moody continued to move toward the Italian galleries as Carasi yelled, "See you in the Staff Caf!" in his wake.

Theirs was a band of four: Moody Russell, Joe Carasi, George Sugarman, and Bill Faden, the Younger (Bill Faden, the Elder managed the custodians). They were the rock stars of the Operations team, smart and specialized in their crucial role.

The four of them had a glittering cool that hung upon their diverging frames. Moody, a tall slab of a man, led the team with wisdom and the longevity of thirty-two years as a lamper. The wiry Carasi served as the sharp fool, quick and jabbing with his spiraling neighborhood humor. Sugarman was the gentle giant, precise and tender within his spongy mass, swollen nose, and cloudy glasses. And Faden, the Younger—and the youngest—played the handsome joiner, game for any twinkling fun. They all shared Moody's crippling fear of the dark, understood, but never mentioned, as their common plague.

The lampers landed at their Staff Caf table at 9:30, trays piled and stomachs ready. They began as usual: a rapid-fire exchange of museum humor that amused them with clapping predictability.

"Hey Moody," Carasi started, nodding toward a table of guards. "How many guards does it take to change a light bulb?"

"Only one," Moody whipped back at him, "But he'll need to do some push-ups first."

"Hey Faden," Moody continued, as an assistant from Development passed, "How many rich guys does it take to change a light bulb?"

"Uh, one to change it, and a Mezz Girl to thank him for making the light possible," Faden thumped, with a wink.

"Hey Sugarman," Faden said, taking up the ball. "How does Dick Trachner change a light bulb?"

"That's classified," Sugarman declared quickly, with faux intensity.

"Hey Joe Carasi," Sugarman said, completing the quartet, "How many curators does it take to change a light bulb?"

"Hooow many?" Carasi exaggerated, as a drawings curator walked by.

"Three. One to change the light bulb, one to show earlier versions that influenced it, and one to say that the changing was actually done by an assistant."

With this daily grace complete, the four bent over their breakfast piles, filling their mouths with the slurping urgency of hungry children. The intimacy of their small family revealed itself when, in the absence of any explanation, Carasi spoke about his sixteen-year-old daughter.

"So, I look at Maria going out the door this morning and it's November and she's got no coat on. So, I say, 'Where's your coat?'—perfectly good question, right?"

Mouths still full, all heads bobbed in agreement, the silent gesture of their amen, high-five, everlasting accord.

"I bought her that nice pink down jacket last year. Cost me a fortune. So, she says, 'Dad, I'm too old for ironic dressing.' Which I hear as 'I'm too old for balsamic dressing.' So, I'm thinking 'Why the hell are we talking about salad?' and she storms out—no coat—and what am I supposed to do? What's ironic about a coat?"

Moody had three children, all out of the house now, and knew the brutal force of teenage rebellion. "Just let her get cold," he counseled, "She'll forget about irony and put on the damn coat."

"Drives me nuts," Carasi responded.

Mouths still full, the heads bobbed again.

"Good sausage today," Faden observed, "It's different."

The heads bobbed steadily now, accompanied by a grunting symphony of approval.

"Turkey, I think," Sugarman added.

Mouths still full, the heads bobbed again.

At 7:25 that night, all the lights went out. Not just in the Met, but across New York City. The plug pulled on the whole apple. A massive blackout.

The visitors had already left, as had most of the staff.

Moody stood before his locker and felt his heart jackhammer with furious speed. His cart was empty, as were the cabinets where they stashed any spare glow.

No light, no escape, nowhere.

His whole life had been structured to avoid this very moment.

The safety bulbs hadn't even switched on. Immediately, the syrupy black of threat, and silence, and unknown everything, coated every crevice of space, every unseen wall, every lurking, pounding, breath-crushing inch before him, thick and trembling like some panicking crowd, despite his isolation.

The door will crack open.

The monster will rage.

The echo will roar.

There was only one place that might rescue Moody. But it would mean crossing the museum, plodding through the ebony swamp of galleries to find his salvation. He would aim for that place like a bull's-eye, knowing that the path of his shivering arrow would not, could not, be straight.

Moody's quaking fear tripped him forward, heaving and unsteady. He staggered into the void as if his boots were two binding weights. The torrent of blackness showered upon him with the might of a gale wind as he trudged across the limestone floors. A long-forgotten howl clamored in his mind, and he slammed his eyes shut as if to squeeze the noise out of his head.

Jumping shadows hinted that other bodies rustled on the edges of Moody's trail, but he couldn't register them as anything solid or real. He prowled onward like a wolf in winter, sniffing with desperation to find scraps for his survival.

His path followed the map of his memory. So many times he had taken this same route, quick and nimble during his happy rounds, never registering its length or snaking turns. His bones finally took over, pulling him right and left and up and forward, through Africa and ancient Greece and Byzantium and then gliding into fifteenth-century Italy.

He turned the corner and there they were, all three of them, stuffed in the Studiolo like a clown car. Moody entered and saw what he had hoped: an impossible stream of warm Italian light still shone through the window and formed a long rectangle on the tile floor. Within that miracle, Carasi, Sugarman, and Faden sat like cats on a windowsill, purring with relief in the Renaissance sun. Moody joined them on the floor and felt the light revive him as it smothered the static charge of his twitching nerves.

Renewed in the persistent glow and soothed by its inconceivable presence, they stayed clustered in silence, relieved in unison, unquestioning of this singular exception to the consuming darkness. Still anxious, Moody broke the noiseless reverie.

"You ever see what this guy looked like?" he asked the others.

"What guy?" Sugarman responded, welcoming the distraction.

"The guy who had this room built?" Carasi asked, joining in the collective diversion. "Wasn't he the Duke of Monte Carlo, or something?"

"Montefeltro," Moody corrected.

"Right, Montefeltro," Carasi agreed.

"Hey Joe Carasi," Faden interrupted with tense humor, "Isn't he a cousin of yours from Staten Island?"

"Yeah, well you should see the nose on this guy, Montefeltro," Moody said to steer the conversation back to his original question; he had seen a picture of Piero della Francesca's famous portrait of Montefeltro.

"Like a Mafia hit man who lost one too many fights. You know those noses that have a ledge at the bridge, like you could rest your beer on it?"

"Oh, like Georgie here," Carasi interjected, "Gogo, what do you keep on that monster beak when you're not wearing those filthy glasses? Leftovers? Snacks?"

"Hey Moody Russell," Sugarman said, ignoring Carasi, and now speaking with a Staff Cafeteria calm, a tone of consoling normalcy. "How many plastic surgeons does it take to change a light bulb?"

Moody knew Sugarman purposefully ignored Carasi's insult to seize deftly on the thematic opening. In that moment, some cardinal reflex took hold, restoring the essential blocks of their constructed world.

"Just one, Sugarman," Moody replied, smiling, "But he'll also want to do something about your nose."

OBJECT LESSON

We protect them and save them and study them, all the while knowing that they think they're protecting us, saving us, studying us. "We" are the art, the evidence, the beauty that these walls are built around and that these lights proclaim important. Objects made of everything, anything: yes, paint and marble, bronze and gold, glass, silver, paper, clay, but also steel and ribbons, mud and hair, wood, wire, and bones. We come from everywhere: tombs and closets, palaces and studios, floors and ceilings, fortresses and temples, sometimes with parts of those places still clinging to us. Because so often we were removed by someone, somewhere, when that someone couldn't wait, or we couldn't stay.

"They" are our minders, men and women with a mothering, smothering kind of love for us. They fret over our every inch, every scratch, every wound, every questionable repair. They polish us like it's the school play, every day. Our big moment for the world to see what beaming, glossy children we are.

Every piece of us is testimony: Whose eye chose that shape, whose hand made that line, whose mallet carved that bump? Show us what happened, they beg, so we'll know.

Well, mamas, there's been some mileage since we were made, some action, in slow drips and big splashes. Glory, war, revolution, the tilts of taste and the swags of renaissance. Some dark, dark ages, too. Empire to dirt in the course of a millennium. Slices cut into our sides to fit us into a new room. A century in a cardboard box, wood-worms drilling like some unscratchable itch. The god-damn vacuum cleaner banging into our legs. Light bulbs!

Shit *happened*. We show them what we can. The rest they guess, and they dig for it—sometimes actually get out the shovel and *dig* for it.

Of course, they have their own dramas, with their delicate fears, their skyscraper egos, and their cracked and broken hearts. We help them when we can, jump into the museum, cradle them the way they cradle us, as if a single breath could crush them. But that mortality business is byzantine stuff, so many knotty roads and intricate pieces.

Survival is a funny business, too. A losing game. Literally. They love us, and we lose them all. The ones who made us, the ones who gave us, the ones who sat down and played with us, the ones who held us, or just laid eyes on us. The ones who bought, traded, and sold us. Cleaned us, redeemed us, brought back the sheen on us. Loved us. Learned everything there is to know about us.

Imagine how many reflections that ancient mirror has seen? Now imagine, *imagine*: Every one of them. Dead. Gone.

But we live on. We are the proof, sticky but silent, hanging on that wall, standing on that pedestal. The proof that anyone was ever there at all.

PAPERCUTS

Walter turned the corner by the ancient dumbwaiter. It was 5:00 AM and his shift had ended. He loved when he was assigned the night shift, particularly this time of day in the serenity of the museum's basement. He walked the hallways to a silent rhythm, the pace of those who had preceded him for a century, and those who would arrive after him, starting their day in just a few hours. He thought of the lemon cake he would bake when he got home, a relaxing ritual in the solitude of his apartment. He would smell that tart, sugary aroma as he sat on his sofa watching TV and anticipating the thick sleep that would soon take hold.

These thoughts were interrupted, and Walter slowed down, surprised by the small pile he saw on the concrete floor. As a custodian, Walter instinctively noticed things that looked out of order, but this was different. He didn't fully grasp what he saw until he got closer, but he realized immediately that the mound of plaid and denim was something fragile and broken.

When he reached it, his breath pulled in sharply, an inhale of shock, followed by the weighted exhale of genuine grief. It was the small body of a staff member, a guy who Walter only knew as the Rubber Band Man. Walter always saw him in that same spot in the basement, diligently organizing the paper Met shopping bags in front of the wall of stacked boxes.

Walter felt for a pulse and confirmed what he already knew. The corpse was curled around itself like a puppy sleeping in a stream of sunlight. The Rubber Band Man looked as he always did: frail, sprightly, but in a ghostly way, with long strands of thin hair pulled away from his face and bound by hundreds of rubber bands into a stiff rod extending from the nape of his neck down his back. His face was the translucent ivory of a polychromed statue of a saint, its surface creased with a life's worth of effort and concentration; his shriveled hands, mapped with gray veins that pushed below his skin like a fragile root system. His eyelids were closed, two moths' wings hung upon the serene and aged face.

Walter knelt down and gently held the Rubber Band Man's head in his hands for a moment—at once a greeting and a farewell—an unspoken "It's ok, I've got you" between strangers. Without thought, Walter scooped the body into his powerful arms, as much to relieve it from its current state as to initiate any other action. He was disarmed by its lightness and the direct sensation of bones through cloth. It felt like the muslin bag of wooden blocks he used to keep in his locker for his son.

He carefully crossed the museum through the basement's winding passages and automatically headed to the Sentry Booth—more than three blocks away—the only place that would be occupied that early in the morning. From the security cameras, it looked as though he were carrying a small load of laundry.

Walter found the loneliness of this singular procession heartbreaking, and felt the wet path of a tear slip down his cheek and land in a small, salty puddle on his lower lip. He didn't even know the Rubber Band Man's name.

The Met mourns rigorously. Not to any one god or any group of gods, or according to any doctrine or religion. But along deep, internal traditions, and with carefully tended rites that evolved in a tribal, rather than orthodox, way.

The news of the Rubber Band Man's death arrived in President Lily Martin's office by 8:00 AM, after the ambulance had taken the body away and the police had spoken to Walter. Moving the body complicated things, but it was clear the cause was natural.

By 8:45, a team assembled in the President's Office on the Fifth Floor to start organizing the staff's grief.

Bruno Parker looked to his boss, Dick Trachner, who responded with an imperceptible nod giving

Parker permission to speak. Trachner's control was legendary, exerted from the large, sparsely furnished office he occupied toward the back of the museum. He spoke with similar economy, as if he had been given a set amount of words for a lifetime and, at age sixty-two, was running low.

Parker began, benevolent as always, but a little grave. "The time of death is still undetermined, but the police don't think an autopsy is needed. We're working with Human Resources to identify any family."

The President interrupted; she had a penchant (and skill) for structuring others' mourning, but details were needed. "Wait. Can we back up? What was the guy's *name*? Did *anyone* in this room know him as anything other than the Rubber Band Man? We can't even write an all-staff memo without his name."

"Constantine Srossic," Chief Legal Counsel Martha Driscoll responded. She remained unflappable in the face of all inquiries and was known as "The Velvet Hammer" for the brutal strength that sat just below her pearls.

Driscoll continued, "He was eighty-seven years old. HR sent his papers over. He has worked here since he was nineteen. No family, no contacts on his emergency form."

The President leaned back in her chair. "Constantine Sewersick." She mispronounced his name, making it sound like a disease you caught on the subway. No one corrected her. She seemed wistful all of a sudden, as if giving him an identity filled her with regret for a relationship they'd never had. "So he worked here for fifty-six years..."

"Sixty-eight," Driscoll clarified.

"What?"

"Sixty-eight," she repeated, "He was eighty-seven."

"Right. Whatever. Sixty-eight years. Jesus. That's twice as long as I've been here, and I feel like I should have an accession number on me," the President responded, referring to the number that every work of art is given when it becomes part of the permanent collection. "Where is he now?" she added bluntly.

"Who?" Parker responded, general whereabouts usually being his concern.

"Sewersick."

"Uh, the morgue? The police put him in an ambulance."

More than one person around the table wondered at that moment where this was going. What did she want, an open casket in the Great Hall?

The President's pity for the anonymous man and his solitary life began to swell. She turned to Libby Davenport, head of Development. Death always ended up in the Development Office. "Libby, draft an all-staff memo. Since there's no family, we'll have to handle the arrangements."

To the outside world this commandeering of someone's final wishes might seem strange, even aggressive. For the Met, this was protocol, a part of the museum's familial staff culture.

Davenport knew this, but immediately questioned the directive, concerned with its possible indication of a new policy. Davenport's glass was always half-empty—and possibly made of steel. "OK, but if we do this for this guy—"

"Constantine Srossic," Driscoll repeated, determined to maintain some decorum.

"Fine. Mr. Serosis, the Rubber Band Man, whatever. Are we now required to take this on for everyone? My staff can't handle becoming a funeral parlor for every Tom, Dick, and Harry who drops dead in this museum."

The President understood the concern, having long advocated for firm precedents that could be cited when complaints blossomed. She replied to Davenport with a tone that acknowledged the established guidelines, while at the same time weaving a narrative to justify ignoring them. It was her singular gift to pursue these diverging paths simultaneously.

"Right. I hear you," the President said, "This can't be the thin edge of the wedge, but we're also talking about possibly the longest-standing—well, not standing, anymore—you *know* what I mean. The longest-*serving* employee here. And one that *did* happen to drop dead in our basement."

Out of the corner of his eye, Parker saw Trachner smirk as the President stumbled over her words, at once compassionate and glib. Driscoll looked down and subtly shook her head, dismayed by the repeated use of the phrase "drop dead."

"Fine," Davenport conceded. "But does this guy even warrant an all-staff memo? When Bill Briggs had a heart attack near the fountains, we just ignored it."

"Libby…" The President did not need to say anything further. The *enough* was implied in her headmistress tone.

"Should a staff coffee be arranged for tomorrow?" the head of Special Events asked, from a chair at the edge of the room. She arrived after the meeting had started, and knew that if Trachner was at the table, one did not join without permission.

"Of course," replied the President, missing Davenport's eye-roll and her exaggerated scribble, noting the decision on her pad.

TO: All Staff
FROM: Michel Larousse, Director
RE: Constantine Srossic

September 15, 2004

As many of you may have heard, the Metropolitan's longest-serving employee passed away last night at the Museum. Constantine Srossic was known to all of us as the diligent organizer of the Museum's shopping bags. His role was critical, and his sixty-eight-year tenure demonstrated his unparalleled dedication to the Museum. The boxes in the corridor to the south of the Staff Cafeteria are a monument to his devoted service.

A staff coffee will be held tomorrow morning at 9:00 AM in the Temple of Dendur to recognize Constantine's contributions to The Met. Thank you.

President Lily Martin knew one thing: There was no way that Director Michel Larousse was going to speak at a staff coffee to honor a man who organized shopping bags. Mourning over mini-muffins never went over well with her boss; deploying his baritone for a man partially encased in office supplies would definitely not fly.

She would do it, a sincere address from the museum's distinguished mama lion to the nine hundred staff members who would gather for their fallen colleague.

At exactly 9:00 AM the next day, a multigenerational span of the museum's staff assembled. While no one claimed any friendship with the Rubber Band Man, he stood for something powerful within an institution defined by loyalty—an unspoken code of respect for those who arrived young, worked hard, and stayed for a lifetime. The Met raised these staff members as its own, unwavering in its devotion and accepting of their many eccentricities, rubber bands and all. It protected Constantine Srossic in its cocoon, even if no one knew his name.

President Martin's speaking style, while fluid and sincere, could occasionally tilt toward the macabre, and she was often more direct than her audience expected. She took to the podium like a seasoned politician, elegant but warm, with hair that could challenge a hurricane. She also maintained her skewed pronunciation of the deceased's name, with little consequence other than to wrongly establish his actual name.

"Good morning and welcome. I am pleased to see so many of you here this morning to bid farewell to Constantine Sewersick.

"He was known as the Rubber Band Man, a quiet, humble staff member who wandered our halls for sixty-eight years. The news that he was found dead—by our own Walter Howe—near his enormous pile of shopping bags sent shock waves of disbelief and grief through our museum. We all knew this timeless hero. The kind man who seemed to never leave his special section of the ground floor. For nearly seven decades, the Rubber Band Man had been seen here every day, and now that will never happen again. So many of us will miss his presence: silent, almost mute...but *friendly*...and welcoming to all.

"Constantine Sewersick's legacy will be his bags: a tidy, ordered tribute to his love of the Met. But as the Rubber Band Man, he was also part of something much bigger: a museum that considers its staff family. We work together, and we grow together, we strive and we celebrate together. And now, we mourn together for a colleague who will be long remembered by us all. May you all hold your shopping bags a little tighter today. Thank you."

Applause followed, along with some extended mingling among the crowd in the light-filled space that held the Egyptian temple. These gatherings worked on a primal level for the staff, securing its belief in the bigger ideals of the Met and affirming their place within its ecosystem. Still grappling with these fundamental convictions and their own mortality, they wrapped pastries into folded napkins and smuggled them back to their offices.

Weeks passed, and chaos gripped the museum shops. No one had ever realized the impact the Rubber Band Man had on bag distribution. One shop had to drop postcards into cavernous bags made for books, while another struggled to jam thick art catalogues into paper sacks designed to hold scarves and jewelry. Bottoms tore, handles broke, near empty bags swept across the Central Park sky like so many branded kites. The tourists complained, the New Yorkers wanted refunds, sales plummeted.

At the Weekly Executive Briefing, the report from the Merchandise Manager confirmed the mayhem. "Get a system in place," demanded the President. "This week."

Edith, a young, eager woman who worked in the Merchandise Department, was dispatched to assess and report on the remains of the Rubber Band Man's supplies, with the hope of understanding his routine. It was a tedious task in a particularly dreary part of the museum, but Edith saw the project as an opportunity to stand out among her colleagues. Armed with her master's degree in art history, she would crack the paper bag challenge.

Edith knew that life at the Met had long followed this course: you got your chance, took your shot, and committed yourself to your minor role within the masterpiece. It was like the great studios of the Renaissance masters, she thought. And she was in charge of painting the ankles.

She began by confronting the hill of boxes that the Rubber Band Man had left behind. Overwhelmed before the ten-foot stack in the otherwise barren hallway, she decided that she needed to inventory them first to see what was inside, labeling them as she went. The cartons reached the ceiling in a formation that reminded her of the Egyptian Tomb of Perneb, a high façade constructed in the alternating pattern of a brick wall. It was heavy work, but armed with a Sharpie and a ladder, Edith conquered each row with quick determination.

As she reached the boxes leaning against the back wall, she was surprised to find some of the cartons were fused together. She shook them a bit and realized they were lighter, too. The combined boxes created a broad surface that reached down to the floor and formed a three-foot wide, six-foot high slab. On one edge of the slab was a bound batch of shopping bag handles carefully wrapped in rubber bands to make a new, larger handle attached to the cardboard. Edith pulled on the handle and the boxes swung open on a series of rubber band hinges, a shocking door within the colossal mound.

Beyond the trick box door was a real door, the entrance to a long-forgotten storage room. *Ingenious*, she thought. She assumed the fake door was a humorous response to a mandate that the storeroom always be accessible. Just when the Rubber Band Man was being reprimanded for ignoring the request, he would smile and reveal his clever joke.

Dreading more boxes that would need to be counted, Edith flipped on the light switch, stepped inside, and immediately knew the inventory was over.

She stood inside a marvel: a breathtaking room constructed entirely of white paper.

And not just any room, a miniature octagonal eighteenth-century French parlor, with elaborate three-dimensional carving reproduced through tiny cuts to the paper. About ten feet across, the space was a perfectly balanced Neoclassical triumph. Egg and dart moldings, bound laurel garlands, playful rosettes, swirls of foliage—layers upon layers of decoration, lined up to define every interior detail: surrounding the ceiling, framing another door opposite the entrance, and outlining two recessed areas, one with a paper daybed, and one with a paper desk and what looked like a large cabinet held closed by an elaborate latch. Narrow panels appeared rhythmically within the architecture, circumscribing each section with minutely recreated decorative molding. A cardboard chandelier hung from paper chains, nine illuminated arms around a centerpiece the size and shape of an inverted eggplant.

Edith couldn't help but touch one of the garlands, admiring the meticulous cuts that allowed it to curve and exist in three dimensions. She knocked on a wall and heard the solid structure beyond it. Only two materials had been used to create this wonder: the white interior of Met shopping bags and the corrugated boxes that housed those bags outside the room.

The whole formed a confection of spun sugar. It sat like a vivid memory, tactile and authentic, but also strange and disconnected. Only later would Edith realize that the Rubber Band Man had crafted a reduced version of the 1775 room from the Hôtel de

Crillon in the Wrightsman Galleries. He had left out the elaborate arabesque painting that is the hallmark of the original, and in doing so, captured the room's unheralded architectural achievement.

The daybed fit perfectly into its two-foot deep alcove, its high sides and back adorned with regimented swags, and its front legs topped with little Egyptian heads—all the rage in late eighteenth-century France—their paper faces appearing like mice emerging from a hole. Edith imagined the Rubber Band Man curled on the bed and recalled the rumor she had heard about his position in the hallway when he was found dead. An overwhelming tenderness toward this stranger and his wonderland came over her. He must have known this day would come, the moment when his invisible creation would be found. Had he envisioned this very instant?

A writing desk sat within the opposite alcove. It was elegantly coupled with a low chair featuring tapered legs that ended in outsized scrolls supporting a seat circled by acanthus leaves. The table simulated eighteenth-century mechanical furniture, with a sliding top that revealed a small surface propped up like a painting on an easel; in its original form, it would likely have been a mirror.

Edith opened the drawer of the desk and was amused to find a single object: scissors. She scooped up the tool that had given life to a fantasy, respecting its heft in her hand. As she leaned down to put the scissors back in the drawer, she got a better look at the easel surface. The frame itself followed the restrained design of the desk. But inside the frame, behind a piece of glass, was something genuine and historic: a museum memo from 1963.

THE METROPOLITAN MUSEUM OF ART
NEW YORK 28 N.Y.

March 6, 1963

To All Employees:

More than a few; many, many of the members of the Museum staff and their families could - and should - be singled out for devotion and service to the Museum during the recent weeks of pressure while the Mona Lisa was on exhibition. Some were heroic in their actions and their restraint under provoking circumstances.

To the Captain and the Lieutenants and their
men we wish to express particular appreciation
and pride. The curators and their staffs and
all of the service departments have cooperated
in many noticed and unnoticed directions. With
what the staff of the Junior Museum had to face,
and the telephone operators and the engineers;
they will tell their stories for years to come.
Mr. Noble, Mr. McGregor, Lil Green and her
staff, Membership and Joan Stack and her helpers
have kept the ship from rocking while it shook
from without and within. The augmented sales
force under Mr. Kelleher and his crew dispensed
printed paper, and the Restaurant and Parking
Lot had their dollar problems. By the combined
efforts of the Museum staff 1,077,521 visitors
were able to view the Mona Lisa within the space
of twenty-seven days.

James J. Rorimer
Director

Edith had heard about the momentous loan from
the French government in a docent lecture she once
attended. Da Vinci's masterpiece was shown in the
Medieval Hall against a deep burgundy velvet curtain
in what looked like a puppet theater. People came in
droves, with crowds spilling out of the museum and

stretching for blocks, despite harsh winter conditions. Once inside, visitors were ushered past the painting and encouraged *not* to stop, as armed Marine guards yelled: "Keep the line moving!" "No standing!" "Keep moving!" "Get along!"

The docent had ended with an apocryphal story about a boy who waited in line for hours. When the moment arrived for him to stand before the picture, the boy opened his coat—to show it to his puppy.

There had also been the cartoonish claim that the actual *Mona Lisa* never went back to the Louvre, and what was now on view in Paris was only a copy.

But a painting with its own Secret Service detail doesn't get lost going through the Met. Edith had only seen the sealed door to the legendary Storeroom One, but she knew that every work of art that had ever entered or left the museum went through that sacred space near the basement loading dock. Nothing was ever lost.

The *Mona Lisa* memo was likely the only correspondence that the Rubber Band Man ever received from any Director of the Met during his decades at the museum. It was touching that he kept it for so many years. A memo from Michel Larousse would likely have the same effect on her.

As Edith settled into her discovery, she fixed upon the doors in the room. She tried to open the one opposite the entrance, but it didn't budge; it was only an illusion within the design. She then approached the door behind the desk—the one that seemed to be part of a large cabinet—and unlatched the cardboard handle from the substantial holder that curled around it like a small hand. The door immediately released on its rubber band hinges. It swung open until it hit the back of the desk, which Edith then moved to the side.

As the door stretched fully open, an interior light turned on, illuminating the cabinet's contents resting on a shallow shelf. And there it sat, as iconic and trite as a postcard image, but much bigger and, well, more charismatic.

"What the hell...," she wondered to no one. It was a curious shrine in the otherwise pristine environment, and an odd, hidden tribute to such a clichéd work of art. "I guess he was really excited when that thing came to town...," Edith mumbled to herself, as she looked more closely at the painting.

The picture was unframed, less than two feet across and maybe two and a half feet high—an inch-thick panel simply propped against the recessed wall that had been crafted to make the cabinet. Edith instinctively picked it up and flipped it over expecting to see more cardboard, more illusion. But it was solid: an ancient, worn piece of wood. She remembered reading that sixty-one copies of the *Mona Lisa* existed all over the world. *Maybe sixty-two,* she thought.

On the back, an uppercase letter *H* was written in one hand and the number twenty-nine scrawled in another; "L Joconde" sat like a signature on the upper left. The remains of dried paper tape outlined the edges of the panel and three lines of an old label were stuck along the top section: "des Tableaux à Versailles" in archaic type and the rest "…du Directeur" written in someone's timeworn scribbled French. A red stamp with a crown and fleur-de-lis read MR No. 316.

Two odd shapes were cut from the panel itself, one filled with wood, the other with a strip of linen; they looked like abstract butterflies, stacked and connected vertically by another piece of linen.

Edith turned it over again, confronting the image itself, and almost felt a breeze as the portrait registered in her eyes once more. From the front she could see that the panel was split from the top of the picture, the cleave luckily stopping at the sitter's hairline so as not to corrupt the famous face. The strange butterfly shapes on the back were likely an attempt to address this split. A web of delicate cracks extended over the painting's entire surface.

A sensation glowed from the painting, golden and warm and insistent, a true soul rather than a tired tourist attraction. It hummed with a unity and balance, an intangible clarity that vibrated just below the artist's diffused rendering.

It seemed to carry the weight of centuries.

"Jesus fucking Christ," Edith said, this time loudly. Her heart began to race, signaling both her own confusion and the feeling that she had wandered into something at once deeply poetic and profoundly complicated. She put the painting back briskly, not wanting to get caught with it in her hands. Any scholar could confirm what Edith now instinctively knew: She had just touched the *Mona Lisa*.

How did this happen? What was sitting in the Louvre? Impossible.

But there it was.

For all the magic of the Rubber Band Man's constructed world, this was real.

Edith's first instinct was to leave. She thought irrationally about fingerprints and evidence, the project of counting the bags, and her chance to make a mark. "Well this should do it," she mused, appeasing the competing directions that willfully pushed at her.

She took a deep breath and couldn't help but smile at the cleverness of the whole thing. The quiet revolution of paper, scissors, and the world's most famous painting. A magnificent life devoted to a pure and constant beauty.

Was Constantine Srossic so different from the curators who tended to their galleries with the same love and precision? The painting never actually left the museum.

There was a storm ahead, to be sure. Science and experts would confirm what seemed to burst from the painting unsolicited. There was a tale to be told, a mystery to be solved, and a good chance that no one would give a shit about shopping bags anymore.

But for now, Edith would just sit in Constantine Srossic's paper palace and delight in its miracle—like it was her own private world, her own exquisite dream. A slice through a paper façade, revealing the glorious shape of an anonymous existence. The tender defiance of a tiny giant, tucked deep within the Met's own mountain.

Edith would forever hold this moment like a curator would hold the *Mona Lisa* itself—as something precious and monumental and far bigger than its humble history. That day was the real beginning of her Met career. She would walk along that basement corridor for another twenty-six years, each day cut and folded by the belief that just beyond the museum's worn paths and daily rituals, there lies the possibility of something wholly unimaginable.

ACKNOWLEDGMENTS

It took twelve months to write this book after thinking about it for twenty-three years. I am grateful to the Metropolitan Museum for allowing me a yearlong sabbatical in 2017 to get the words finally out of my head. My earliest supporters were a group of exceptional women who gave me the courage to make that leap: Deborah Needleman, Annabelle Selldorf, Julie Burstein, Rosemarie Ryan, Emily Rafferty, and Andy McNicol.

Along the way, I had many terrific readers: Alice Attie, Deeda Blair, Andrew Bolton, Julie Burstein, Steven Estok, Michael Gallagher, Andrea Glimcher, John Habich, James Kaliardos, Maira Kalman, Christopher

Noey, Russell Piccione, Jennifer Russell, Leanne Shapton, Andrew Solomon, Martin Solomon, and Stephen Yorke. Their encouragement and questions made all the difference.

Hilary Leichter Griffin, my phenomenal editor during my sabbatical year, pushed the text in all the right places and pushed me at all the right moments.

My magnificent publisher, Judith Gurewich, understood the book immediately and has the most finely tuned editorial ear in existence. Reading my book to her over the phone day after day allowed me to see what only she could hear. Her team at Other Press is superb and unrivaled. The amazing John Gall designed the book's cover, nailing it on the first try.

Residencies at the American Academy in Rome and the Shoichi Noma Reading Room at the New York Public Library were crucial during my sabbatical, as were the New York Society Library, the Bobst Library at NYU, and the Met's own Thomas J. Watson Library. The wonderful Kathleen Gerard lent me her son Rupert's room so I could write on Shelter Island.

Even in fiction, the truth is sometimes critical. At the Met, I had the help of Jim Moske and Barbara

File in Archives, where I discovered small details like Jacob Rogers's address and the memo to the staff after the *Mona Lisa*'s visit to the Met in 1963. The memo in "Night Moves" about the guards in the closet is also real and was passed to me by a colleague years ago. The description of Jim Campbell's *Walking Man* video in "The Talent" comes from the outstanding catalog entry written by Doug Eklund, Curator of Photographs, one of the Met's most brilliant minds. And I am grateful to Tom Scally, Buildings General Manager, who generously escorted me through the tunnels beneath the museum, which I had not seen in more than a decade.

If I could thank each individual member of my Met family I would, but you are far too many in number, a sky full of stars. I will always remember the time captured in this book as our own Lake Wobegon days: All the women were strong, all the men were good-looking, and all the children were above average.

And finally, there are no greater champions of this writer than my three Cs. You are my greatest loves and fiercest defenders. Every word is for you.

Visit

www.christinecoulson.com/art

to explore the works of art featured
in *Metropolitan Stories*.